The Deceit Series

Vol 1. Everything That Glitters

The Deceit Series
Vol 1. Everything That Glitters

written by
Edishia Roundtree

To The Old Dee...
You did it.

*Thank you for being a **warrior.***

Table of Contents

Acknowledgment

I don't believe in a "Thank You" when it involves someone or something of substance. To me, those are for things that you expect of others. I however, believe in showing gratuity and appreciation. It hits a little deeper when you appreciate it.

I appreciate those of you that helped pave the way for me to complete and publish my first book. You were my back bone and motivation during times of procrastination and self-doubt. You were my pick me up and inspiration during times I experienced writer's block. You were my boost of energy during times I wanted to sleep at night but there was work to be done. You were my sounding board when nothing sounded right. You were my hype men and women during time's I felt this book was pointless. You were the constructive criticism I needed when I was in over my head…

You were my friends, my family, my partner, my peers and my editors. You were the ones that made this happen. You were my father, **Eddie B** who thoughtfully hand drawn the beautiful cover. You were **Leah**, who was the person that told me to take my short story and make it a novel. You were **Khadijah**, who read as I wrote and told me to keep going. You were the few people I sent excerpts and told me they were ecstatic to read the rest. You were **Melinda**, who let me read to her aloud and pushed me to finish this book in 24 hours after going on a year plus hiatus. You were **Nas**, who has always been my backbone, my king, the one that sees me for more than I see myself, my hype man and my biggest fan. You were **Tahara** and the editing team that made my wrongs right. You were my peers in the military who saw me for more than a sailor. You were the ones who speak success and life into me that keeps me going. You were those who weren't mentioned but your contribution goes unnoticed.

You were the few, the loyal, the homies!

And I appreciate you all!

Preface

"Behind every great novel, is a great struggle dying to be told." - Dee

Before I start, I just want to say, this book almost didn't happen. Even at this very moment as I type this preface, I'm thinking to myself. WOW! I'm really writing a preface almost 3 years later. Does that mean I'm an author now? The thought of that pains my soul because now that I'm here, I'm just proud to say we did it. I did it and it almost didn't happen! This section is going to give you a little insight into the mind of Dee and a few words that's just me saying it's going to be all over the place.

This series is less about entertainment and more so about obtaining peace of mind and freedom for me. Though the Deceit series is sure to be the companion of many lovers of urban novels and African American fictional books (that's me manifesting that you all will love this book). For me, this series represent a constant reminder of where I was and where I am.

"The Deceit Series," was my home away from my current home which was away from home. Let me put this in simpler terms. I served in the Navy for 5 years onboard a ship. During that time, I had found myself drifting into sorrow, misery and depression. While I could have drowned in my sorrow, I decided to create a new place for me to go and get away from reality. As a kid I would always have composition books full of poems and short stories. I had a wild imagination and storytelling served as a way for me to express all that was me. Deceit represents the gray area between where I currently was and where I planned to go. The struggle between knowing you're going to make it someday, trying to enjoy the process and mentally quitting and praying to yourself and the higher power for it to happen any day now. I call that the millennial curse.

This book is a bridge. A tool! A graveled terrain. It's your reminder that no matter where you are, or what you're going through reality is solely based on your perception and you have the power to alter that perception and therefore change your reality.

Though this book is fiction, a lot of it is based on real life scenarios. You may be reminded of a friend, a lover, a long-lost cousin, or yourself. All I'm going to say is don't try any of this at home. I hope this book inspires all to not take what is given on the surface for truth. To believe half of what their shown and only a third of what they're told, especially in this digital age. Prepare your bath, body and soul and get ready to unravel the life of family and friends that represent the epitome of "everything that glitters, isn't goals," my Boss Queen Sistah Shaya once said.

CHAPTER I

"Mommy! Mommy!"

Talyn shoved her mom left and right until she woke her. Tamia woke up startled to the sound of her daughter's voice but relieved when she saw that precious smile on her face. "Are we still going to the zoo today?" Talyn reminded her mommy.

Shit, Tamia thought. She forgot she had told her that she would take her to the Zoo. She had been so busy with work and finally scheduled an appointment with this local designer whom had been giving her a hard time for the past 7 months. The baby sitter was already scheduled to arrive in the next hour. "Of course, baby, mommy has to go to work for a few hours and as soon as I'm done, we're going to the Zoo. Okay?" She asked Talyn as she grabbed her face and kissed her on the lips.

How could she resist that soft convincing smile, and those big beautiful hazel eyes? She resembled every inch of her mother, from her short and thick natural curly hair to her eager and dedicated attitude.

"Eewww mommy that's nasty. You kiss daddy," Talyn was too smart for her own good.

Tamia laughed as she phoned the baby sitter to confirm she was still coming. Fortunately, she was on her way. Tamia was already running late so she picked Talyn up, escorted her to her room on her Princess Tiana carpet and turned the TV on to Frozen. Back to her room she scurried off to get dressed. "Mommy," Talyn screeched! You can never get tired of that voice. Tamia reversed and ran back into her room. Talyn stuck her pinky finger into her mouth and reached out for her mommy to shake, "Pinky promise?"

"Pinky promise," she gave Talyn her word.

She resumed getting dressed. Normally she is on time for everything but this appointment threw her off schedule taking into account Saturdays and Sunday's are usually her off days. It would be really unfortunate if she was late to this appointment. Tamia and her people had been working so hard to book Jarvis Rashad and she finally succeeded. "Alright crazy lady one shot," Jarvis told her and she could not forget that statement. Tamia took pride in her work. The door bell rung just in time, she had just finished getting dressed.

"Talyn!" She yelled up the stairs as she opened the door for the baby sitter. "Hey Cam, thank you again. I know its last minute. I really appreciate you." "No problem Mrs. Suthers, you know I love Talyn." Tamia grabbed her keys off the hook, pressed the auto start button on her 2015 white on white Lexus then continued to the kitchen closet to grab her purse and dashed off to her office. Pulling up to her downtown office and seeing Her Image written big and bold on the top of her building was Tamia's favorite part of each day. Her Image was everything you could imagine. She did it all, but the heart of her business was marketing. Before going inside, she made her morning run across the street to Starbucks. She ordered the same thing every morning: hot Grande White Mocha with whipped cream, caramel drizzle and a warm croissant. Besides seeing her business this also made her morning.

She walked inside, closed her eyes and just stood there soaking up the positive energy. Luckily her assistant was already there setting up. Demetri was the best assistant any business person could ask for. It was as if he was her conscious. Demetri was like Tamia's little brother – or sister, whichever he wanted to be today. The instrumentals were softly bleeding through the walls of the office which set the tone for every morning. The water and basket of snacks were already set up in the middle of the table as well as a variety of soda in the refrigerator. He had her sample marketing profiles laid out all over the table for her potential client to view. There was nothing more Tamia could ask of him.

"Someone had a good night last night, huh?" Demetri giggled. "Nooooo, I woke up late and honestly I was woken up by Talyn asking about the Zoo," she answered, "can you believe that." "I had a feeling with this sudden change in schedule that you may have run a little late." "You're a life saver De." "Tell me about it." They laughed. "Oh, by the way, did you speak with Jarvis yet?" she confirmed. "Mm Jarvis," he looked up to the ceiling and gazed into space with eyes of lust, "Nope he didn't answer. He'll be here boss don't worry." "Oh, I know he will," Tamia said with not a worry in her heart.

Demetri walked out of the conference room and in seconds he turned around yelling he's here. He walked over to the mirror and began freshening up. "Demetri, really," Tamia laughed. "What? You never know." Demetri laughed then proceeded back to his desk to greet Jarvis.

There he stood: tall, dark and handsome. His demeanor reflected confidence as he blessed the room with his presence. His attire spoke hood wealth: gold chains enwrapping his solid built neckline, rings on pretty much all of his fingers and to top it off he had a big gold Rolex on his wrist. From the looks of it, you could presume he was dressed in his own clothing line P.A.G. (Pride and Glory) with matching Asics on his feet. Jarvis was a young entrepreneur with hopes of simply surviving but no ambition to become famous. He walked in with what seemed to be a bodyguard considering his demeanor but then again *why would a local clothing designer need a bodyguard*. He looked around admiring her office.

"Hello, Welcome to Her Image. How are you today Mr. Rashad?" Demetri greeted the client.

"I'm good, thanks," he began walking around as if looking for something, "Is Ms. Suthers here?"

Tamia walked out of the conference room and instantly brightened the space. Head held high with poise strutting in her fitted Marc Jacobs pants suit as her red bottoms clicked against the marble floor, she brushed her hair off her shoulders, buttoned her blazer and stuck her arm out to shake his hand. He took a step back and looked her up and down in awe. *Damn. The things I'd do to her*, he thought to himself. "Hello Mr. Rashad, thank you for coming in today. I will not disappoint you." She turned away and directed him and his team into the conference room. Tamia didn't waste any time. She was all about her business. One thing that she was confident about was her ability to convince others that they needed her.

"Now all I ask is that you give me about 15 minutes of your time and I promise you will not regret it."

"I'm here aren't I?" He sat back in his seat ironically intimidated by this ambitious woman. Tamia did not allow his arrogance to faze her.

Tamia presented her ideas and flipped through the images she had gathered on her smart board. She walked around to the side of the table explaining all of the documents Demetri had laid out for him. "The possibilities are endless," Tamia was ecstatic regarding their potential. Demetri walked into the room, "Excuse me. Your husband is on the phone."

"Thank you, Demetri, I'll be right there..."

"Do you have something better else to do?" Jarvis was obviously feeling some type of way. The cocky bodyguard looking guy finally spoke up, "We'll just have a lawyer look over it and get back with you." His voice was way softer than expected. "That's perfectly fine," Tamia said as she shook his hand.
He gathered the portfolio and proceeded to leave. "I appreciate it; I'll give you a call."

Darnell was calling to see if his wife wanted to meet up for lunch. Considering her meeting was over she took him up on his offer. "Okay, Demetri. Thank you for everything today. I believe we may have pulled it off." Tamia shared with a boost of assurance. "That's what's up, so I'm guessing it went well?" Demetri asked as he looked down at his phone smirking. "It went well, I can tell he's still trying to put up a front and be stubborn though, but I see straight through it," she notices him smirking and acknowledges. "What are you blushing about?"

"Oh nothing," he continues smiling, staring down at his phone, "by chance are we done for today." "Yes, Demetri enjoy your night with let me guess...... David?" David was Demetri's new boo thang he rants about all day every day. "Actually, I met someone new Ms. Know it all." Demetri was like Tamia's little brother from another mother. They were fairly close with regard to their positions. "Look at you! Well, Darnell and I are heading to lunch. Lock up and I'll see you Monday."

Tamia already had her car running for her to be on her way to her husband. She hadn't seen him since prior to bed last night, taking into account he gets up early for work every morning. Darnell had just recently opened his own law firm; in the heart of downtown Jacksonville, after enduring a demotion where he recently worked. He obviously did not allow that to deter him rather than providing an excuse as well as motivation for him to reside and start his own firm. With several associates at his beck and call; Tamia's best friend Salina being one, business was better than he could hope for.

She walked into one of her favorite bakeries, Panera Bread, at which her husband invited her to grab a quick bite to eat during his lunch break. Her husband was sitting there looking handsome as always awaiting her arrival with her favorite salad ready for her to devour. She attempted to sneak up behind him but before she knew it her scent gave her away and her husband quickly turned around and kissed her on the lips. They shared a laugh as she sat down directly in front of him.

"Hello my Queen how was work?" he greeted his wife the usual. Tamia went on sharing what she felt was good news regarding her potential client Jarvis Rashad. Darnell was not familiar with the name but he did recall seeing the acronym P.A.G. throughout the city. He knew his wife was good at what she does but unfortunately, he did not like it when she "wasted her hard-earned degree on local hood rats." Tamia was the type to have faith in everyone and with the drive to become a top marketing agent in Florida she did not mind taking risks because with great risks comes great results.

She inadvertently looked down at her watch and noticed it was quickly approaching 1 pm. She forgot she had promised Talyn that she would take her to the zoo. "Baby I forgot I told Talyn I would take her to the zoo today since I was supposed to be off," she informed him sorry to cut their date short, "Can you come?" "Sorry baby I have to head back to the office, last minute work to finish. But I'll be home before you know it," he smiled and kissed her on the lips. "I love you," she grabbed his face and instantly stuck her tongue down his throat massaging the inside of his mouth. Darnell backed away smirking while biting his lips. "I miss you too boo, I'll be home tonight to finish where you left off." He grabbed her hand and walked outside to her car where she had parked directly behind his 2015 black and chrome Jaguar with tinted windows to add to the theme. They both had just recently purchased new vehicles as gifts to themselves in light of their advancements. Like the gentleman that he is, he opened the door for her and kissed her one last time as she stepped into the car. "I love you!"

Tamia lied in bed, disinclined to get up and get dressed for dinner with the girls after last night. Darnell arrived home later than expected and as mad as she could have been she didn't have time to think about it after waking up to her husband's tongue against her thighs. She immediately awoke sighing with bliss. If there was one thing that her husband was good at besides making his family happy, it was making his wife cum. He bit her panties and slid them down her legs gathering them into his hand, throwing them onto the floor and instantly began to please her. The arch in her back and the sound of her crying out for mercy turned Darnell on more and more, he could definitely satisfy his wife with his tongue alone. He grabbed her by her petite waist and pulled her body closer to his face savoring the taste and inhaling the sweet vanilla aroma that aroused his sense of smell.

"Oh, baby yes, right there, right there," she hinted for him not to move. He removed his mouth for a matter of seconds and you could tell Tamia was not too happy about that. He took his finger and gently penetrated her pussy as he continued to lick her clitoris. Tamia grabbed his head as if to push him away from her, she had reached her climax. Her legs began to shake so hard, the feeling took over her body as she unintentionally squeezed Darnell's head with her thick thighs. He popped up from between her legs and began to slowly climb on top of her. He grabs hold of her pierced nipples massaging them with his fingers, while dragging his tongue up her stomach mindful not to miss a spot. He inserted his long, thick and brown manhood into her pussy. She moaned loudly into her husband's ear, devouring the moment while he took control of her body.

"Don't wake TT baby," he laughed, "here, bite the pillow." Tamia was not hearing anything that he was saying; she was too high for her to come down. As he slowly began to pull himself out of her, she grabbed him by his ass and pressed herself against him ensuring to receive it all. He continued making love to his wife in and out, around and around, round for round until suddenly she released her ecstasy all over him for the third time. "I love you, all of you," he reminds his wife with such passion as if she doesn't already know. Her head on his chest, she panted away attempting to sober up after the intoxicating pleasure she had abstained. She quickly regained consciousness so to speak; she wanted her husband to feel the same things she did. She took her shaking hands and wrapped them around his big dick and slowly licked up the sides. She gently took all of him into her mouth as he pushed deep and hard wanting to feel the back of her throat. She began looking seductively into his piercing eyes trying her hardest not to gag; he bit his lip, jerked and gave her everything that he had that day and she accepted. That night he held her close and tight to his chest as if never to let go. She fell asleep in his arms like a baby.

Salina finally arrived to the restaurant late as always. Tonya and Tamia expected as much and for that reason they weren't even upset. For every group of friends there must always be one that insists on showing up everywhere fashionably late as if to make a bold entrance of some sort. The girls plan to meet up at least twice a month to catch up on the latest. Once upon a time they were a crew of four, but everyone with the exception of Salina disassociated themselves with Jacqueline soon after they found out she had a lot to say about them behind closed doors. Why is Salina still friends with her? Well, ironically, she didn't have any negative thoughts about Salina. It's weird, right? But then again it made a lot of since considering her and Salina were friends first; Jacqueline was the one that introduced us to Salina. They both cheered together in high school and met back up in Jacksonville after Salina graduated from college.

Upon graduating from law school Salina took on an internship at Darnell's new law firm. Tamia being a good friend thought it was only right for her to refer her best friend to her husband for work. She only had a few weeks left and she would either continue to work their full time or start at a different firm. But knowing her I'm sure she'd want to continue working with Darnell because she'd feel she'll have it easy. Everything was apparently going great so far. Tonya on the other hand was a Registered nurse over at the family clinic off Emerson Street. She had three children and a divorced husband whom she can't seem to totally separate from. Unfortunately, Tonya never made it back to school to accomplish her ultimate goal of becoming a Doctor after her second baby. But of course, she still plans to, eventually.

"Nice of you to join us," Tonya snarled.

"I couldn't find anything to wear." Salina thought of the first excuse that came to her head. If that is the real reason, she must can never find anything to wear being that she's late everywhere. Even work. The waiter returned to the table briefly after noticing the guest that they mentioned they were waiting for, to return to take their orders. "And what will you have to drink ma'am?" The waiter asked.

"You if you're on the menu... Michel," Salina bit her bottom lip seductively, putting herself out there as bait. The waiter just laughed and continued around the table getting the rest of the lady's appetizers. She stopped him before he could walk away and asked that he get her his favorite drink.

"Really, Salina," Tamia asked regarding her flirty comment towards the waiter, "I think you made him uncomfortable, then calling him by his name like you just know him like that. You are something else I tell you." Salina was known for being the promiscuous and flirty friend. 'Situationships' were just that to Salina, relationships that quickly transpired into regrettable situations. "What, he was cute," she spoke on her actions. "Whatever," Tamia changed the subject, "Tonya, you and the hubby still mingling?" "Of course, we are," Tonya shook her head embarrassed because even she knew what she was doing wasn't healthy for herself or her family.

"Why don't you guys just get back together?" Salina asked obviously not taking into account their dreadful past together. Rodney, whom was Tonya's ex-husband, cheated on her and got another woman pregnant. He pleaded his case, she took him back and like a foolish man he cheated again. Tonya couldn't see herself having sex with another man nor introducing her children to someone else taking into consideration he was her first. Just the thought alone was unbearable.

Tonya and Tamia both in sync looked at Salina surprised that she would even ask such a thing. "Look, I know it doesn't make any since but I want my children to be raised by both their mother and father." "You know you guys can do that without sleeping together right?" She was one to talk. Salina just knew all of the right things to say. "You better just find you one of these young brothers to get you right. Trust me you'd be surprised they do it better than men our age these days; must be something in the breast milk." As mad as Tonya wanted to get, she couldn't help but laugh at the comment Salina made. "Girl you are a predator!" They all shared a laugh. "Don't lie and say you haven't thought about it?" Salina gazed around the table awaiting the truth. "There is nothing I can do with a young boy besides help build his credit," Tamia expressed.

The waiter returned to the table with their drinks and appetizers as the ladies continued to joke and laugh about Salina's cougar like dealings. "Now isn't that the truth." Tonya agreed. "Mozzarella sticks, a shrimp and spinach dip, and last but not least, a chef salad with Italian dressing." He passed the appetizers around to everyone. "Is there anything else I can get you ladies?" Tonya looked around the table to confirm they were all good. They nodded their heads so she replied, "No thank you, good for now." "And for you ma'am," he turned to Salina. She smirked at him as she admired his athletic built body. "I guess that's nothing." He stated as he walked away.

"He knows he wants me."

"Oh my gosh! You need to stop it Salina. You're going to scare the poor baby away from our table." Tonya was getting fed up with her shenanigans. "You're just mad because I still got it and you're stuck with the same cheating ass ex-husband." Salina rolled her eyes. This statement left an awkward silence at the table. Soon after, Tamia broke the silence with her latest news regarding work. She was still excited about her meeting with Jarvis. They continued their dinner although the tension was still in the air between Tonya and Salina. Their friendship has always been on the rocks being that Tonya doesn't quite support Salina's immoral like ways. She was what Tonya would call 'loose'. The waiter returned with the checks. Salina thought it was funny to leave her phone number on the signature line of her receipt. Guess she really was interested in him.

Tamia was relieved to walk into her lavender smelling home after a tense dinner with the ladies. Tamia had noticed that Tonya's facial expression and body language appeared bothered after Salina's nice comments, that she decided to text her checking on her. She hung her keys on the hook and was immediately drawn towards a note on the island table that read:

"TT and I decided to have our own little dinner date. Be home shortly. Xoxox Poose and Goose."

He's so cute, she thought. Poose and Goose was Darnell's nickname for him and the baby. He was Poose and as you can guess Talyn was Goose because she loves to chase him everywhere, he goes. She blushed, grabbed the note and attached it to the magnet on the refrigerator. A delightful bubble bath was calling her name. Tamia just wanted to relax after all the pressure she was feeling after work and that dreaded dinner. Demetri reminded her countless times today that he hadn't heard from Jarvis as well as her concern for her friend Tonya. Tamia wasn't usually the worrying type but Demetri was feeling apprehensive and it was without a doubt starting to rub off on Tamia, bearing in mind it had been about two weeks since she had met with Jarvis.

Tamia felt sore as if she had been lifting weights and just wanted to be to herself and relax. As she undressed, she found herself fascinated with the smell of sweet pea and strawberries coming from her bathroom. To her surprise, the bathroom was lit by candles alone; her bathtub filled with bubbles accompanied by rose petals, a purple laced lingerie two piece on the hook, a wrapped box on the toilet seat, and furthermore her iPod (playlist selected) awaiting her permission to play. She opened the wrapped gift box and laid her big hazel eyes upon a pair of the most beautiful Steve Madden shoes she'd recently seen in a magazine. What was the occasion, she wondered? Her husband knew her all too well. It was as if he could feel her uneasiness, or then again it could just be the fact that he knows her friends have a way of changing her mood. That's not in a positive manner either, disappointingly. She sat in a daze momentarily appreciating the scenery, consuming the aroma, and thinking of her perfect life. It was something about that moment that tranquilized her and put her mind at peace. Suddenly she snapped out of it and proceeded into the Jacuzzi tub. She just rested there for at least twenty minutes before she was suddenly interrupted at the sound of the living room door.

Poose and Goose were home.

Darnell slowly poked his head into the bathroom door with admiration of the sight of his woman washing herself. "I'll be back to join you," he said as she blew him a kiss. Tamia was looking forward to thanking her husband for being so generous. Talyn was already 3 steps ahead of her father as she was getting ready for bed. "Thank you daddy for pizza, don't tell mommy okay?" Tamia didn't like for Talyn to eat fatty foods on weekdays. Saturdays were her family's cheat day as they would go out for dinner and eat whatever their appetite desired. "Promise," Darnell smiled at his princess and left her room.

By the time Darnell made it back to their master bedroom, Tamia was already draped in her new attire sitting at the foot of their California King sized bed in anticipation of her king's arrival. Darnell just stood there at her feet, glaring into her eyes saying more than any words could express. She grabbed his belt and pulled him towards her. He took a step back joking with her. She would not let go of his belt. She tried again to loosen his belt and this time she was successful. He unbuttoned his shirt and allowed it to fall off his shoulders as she turned him around and threw him on the bed. Tamia didn't even allow Darnell to get fully undressed before she took possession of his dick into her hands. She allowed her mouth to get as moist as possible and then she began to drool onto his hard on. Within a split second she had taken him into her mouth and pleased him with every ounce of appreciation in her body. Darnell was unquestionably satisfied. He was ready to make love to her. Tamia finished her contractual obligation and attempted to go to sleep as if nothing had ever taken place. Darnell was baffled. He wanted more. "Thanks again baby I really needed that after my day," she said in a soft and thankful tone. Darnell was not accepting defeat. He wanted more.

He picked Tamia up from the bed and escorted her to the shower with him where he finished where she had left off.

CHAPTER II
Business as Usual

She just sat there staring off into space, phone in her right and hand on her chin. She looked confused, lost. Demetri walked in observed her appearance and decided to just let her think. Although business was not what she sought; Tamia had plenty of clients to keep her busy for at least the next year. She sat there for a matter of minutes contemplating whether to give him a call or not. This was not her usual self, but then again good business required a follow up. More than anything else the fact that Tamia remained consistent and finally got through to Jarvis she was taken back that he had not called her back yet. She grabbed his phone card and began to dial his number then suddenly something came over her. He'll call, she told herself. Tamia knew that she and her employees did a hell of job on his portfolio; there was no way he could pass up the opportunity to work with her.

"Welcome to Her Image, nice to see you again Mr. Rashad. Tamia?" Demetri was astounded himself to see Jarvis back in the building after all of the negative energy he rubbed off on Tamia. Tamia overheard Demetri greet Jarvis and found herself smiling with relief. Demetri escorted Jarvis to

Tamia's office. "I have Jarvis Rashad here to see you," Demetri opened the door half way and Jarvis took the initiative of just walking in. Demetri smiled after observing what was behind Jarvis back and turned back to his desk.

"Hello, Mr. Rashad. What brings you today?" As if she didn't already know. Guess she just wanted to hear the words come out of his mouth for reassurance. As Jarvis sat down, he placed flowers and a gift bag onto Tamia's desk.

"You know why I'm here."

"I thought I did. I'm flattered but you must have the wrong idea. I'm married Mr. Rashad..." and before she could complete her statement Jarvis chimed in. "No, no." he laughed, "I just want to thank you for your work. I was very pleased with what I saw and I want us to work together." Jarvis opened the gift bag and unfolded a P.A.G. shirt for her. "I brought one for your secretary too." She laughed discomfited by her assumptions, "Oh my. I appreciate it." She placed the shirt against herself to check the size. "I think this will fit just fine. What about the flowers?" She was obviously still feeling uncomfortable by the flowers. "That's just my way of saying thank you. I didn't mean anything by them. Thought you women just liked flowers, my bad." Jarvis grabbed the flowers and sat them on his lap to get them out of her view. "So, what's next?" he asked. "Fashion show," she introduced excited by the sound of it. "We invite other local designers, 93.3, the newspaper, magazines, big names, everyone. We introduce your line to a wider area than just Jacksonville and wait for the calls to start coming in." "I like your confidence." He smirked. "So, when do we start?" "Well first I need to see those contracts you're hiding over there with a signature on them." Jarvis revealed the documents from the manila folder and placed them directly in front of Tamia. "Now, when do we start?" Tamia giggled admiring Jarvis's consistency and sarcasm.

Tamia did not want to waste any more time. Her time was as valuable as her money, and with the last few weeks gone down the drain she was ready to get the show on the road. She called Demetri into the room and updated him on their newest project. Demetri was excited, fashion was his forte'. "I'll get right on it," he accepted the task and like he stated he began making calls. Demetri was the perfect person for this project. Although, Tamia knew that she could leave it all in Demetri's hands for a successful outcome she wanted to be a part of the vision. Jarvis insisted that he would do his part and create more pieces for the show as well as bring in more pieces for them to view. Jarvis clothing line was targeted mostly towards inner city children who typically can't afford the finer brands such as polo or guess. Tamia loved the concept. He made a wide variety of clothes, from little girls to grown men. In that moment

Jarvis felt his dream becoming more alive than he ever imagined.

As Tamia scrambled through her desk looking for her phone book, she stopped for a second and realized that she was so excited she was moving too fast. Have you ever been so excited about something that it just suddenly took over your every being and caused you to overlook something that was directly in your face the whole time? Well, that's the state Tamia was currently in. She grabbed a to-do list off of her organizer and began writing a schedule of things to do in order to guarantee the success of the P.A.G. fashion show. Tamia arose from her desk and left her office, "Demetri, grab Micah, Sharaine and Lisa and come into the conference room." Without hesitation Demetri ended his phone call, called to the workstations in the back and followed behind Tamia into the conference room. Tamia bid Jarvis goodbye as she continued her business with her employees.

"Okay here's the plan," Tamia posted a list on the smart board for everyone to view. "Now, everyone take a second to look over and choose an assignment. If anyone happens to choose the same job you guys can either work together or settle it. And if that doesn't work, which I'm sure it will, I will just choose for you." "What about the models?" Micah chimes in inquiring for a reason other than business considering the look on his face as well as his tone. Micah was the technical expert at Her Image. He was in charge of marketing over the internet, and he was damned good at it. "Mr. Rashad, Demetri and I will take care of the models," Tamia already had a plan for that. "Why can't I help?" He obviously wouldn't give up.

The room laughed in sync at Tamia's response, "Demetri has better taste."

As everyone took possession of their assignment and headed back for work, Tamia decided to let everyone off and start fresh tomorrow. Everyone was excited to hear that, they sped off back to their work stations, packed up, and headed home before Tamia had a chance to realize it was only 10 o'clock. "You must have plans today?" Demetri asked curious. "No, I'm just excited. It's a lot to take on during a day's notice; therefore, I felt it would be best to just start fresh tomorrow. Plus, I don't want to hear anyone's mouth when we're all working late to get this done. Would you like to stay here?" Demetri turned around as if he never even asked a question and went about his day. Tamia just stood there and laughed. She straightened up the conference room and went back to her office to grab her belongings.

Tamia decided at the last minute to stop by Darnell's office to take him and Salina some lunch given that today was supposed to be a long day for everyone in his office; his previous case didn't go as planned in court. As she walked into the firm with their subs from Firehouse, Tamia was greeted by Darnell's secretary whom was aware of Tamia's relation and let her in. Darnell was in his office conversing with Salina who sat directly across from him when Tamia entered. Salina turned around quickly as she observed the expression on Darnell's face when he saw his wife walk in. "Hey love." She said ignoring Salina's presence. Tamia was still a little upset with Salina after their recent dinner. She hadn't talked to her since but regardless she was her friend. "I brought you something to eat."

"Thanks Mia," he appreciated the nice gesture and got up to hug her. Salina arose in unison and greeted her friend also. "I brought you something also," Tamia informed Salina as she handed her the sub. "Could you excuse us?"

"Thanks girl. I was starving," she took the food and exited Darnell's office.

Like the gentleman he was, he pulled out the chair and gestured for his wife to sit. Darnell didn't waste any time devouring his meal. "You must've been hungry?" Tamia asked observing how quickly he ate his sub. "I was," he said with his mouth full of food. Tamia hated it when people talked with their mouth full. Before she could even say a word, Darnell could foresee her response to his ill-mannered actions so he stopped her in her tracks and apologized. "So, what happened with the case?" she was interested in knowing. "Baby I really don't want to talk about it right now because that motherfucker pissed me off. Let me just finish up all this paperwork and I'll be home later and fill you in, okay?" Darnell was furious regarding the case; you could see it all over his face as soon as she mentioned it. Tamia got up from her seat, walked around the desk and began to massage Darnell's shoulders.

"Don't let it stress you. I'm sure you guys will get through it. Remember everything happens for a reason." Darnell just looked up and puckered his lips asking for a kiss. Tamia kissed him, grabbed her purse and left. She stopped at the door and turned around, smiled and said, "What do you want for dinner?" That was a rhetorical question because whenever she asked him what he wanted the answer was always the same: 'Steak, baked macaroni and cheese, broccoli with cheese, corn bread, and Cajun rice.' That was Darnell's favorite meal.

"You already know. Can you grab another bottle of white Pinot Grigio also and some Remy Martin?" he asks enthusiastically. "Of course," She says softly as she closed the door.

On Tamia's drive to the grocery store she

decided to stop by Talyn's school and pick her up early. Although, Talyn is usually in the way while her mom is cooking Tamia figured today, she'd actually allow her to assist. Once they got home, Tamia got straight to the point and began prepping the steak. As she allowed the steak to marinate for a few hours she insisted on helping Talyn with her homework. "Talyn, do you have any homework today," her mother asked. "Yes mommy. But can I do it after I finish playing the game?" "No, Talyn. You will finish your homework first then you can play the game, deal?" As much as Talyn did not want to agree to those terms she knew she didn't have a choice. They finished up her homework then Tamia went to the kitchen to check on the meat. While Tamia started the rest of the food she sat Talyn down at the counter and allowed her to mix the batter for the corn bread. Once complete, she ensured it was mixed well then inserted it into the oven. In the meantime, as they waited for the food to finish they played Dance-Dance together. Once the food was complete, Tamia and Talyn made the table and took their showers while awaiting the arrival of Darnell.

Tamia could hear Darnell's car pull up outside and instantly she felt butterflies. She was excited that her man had arrived home after the stressful day she knew he had. He walked into the house and immediately slouched onto the couch he was so exhausted. "Baby are you ready to eat?"

Tamia asked. "Yes!" Darnell exclaimed. Tamia walked over to the kitchen and began making her husband's plate. Typically, they sit at the dining table as a family and eat dinner but Tamia figured she'd make an exception this one time considering the circumstances. Tamia sat Talyn down at her personal table and they joined him in the living room for dinner. Darnell thanked his wife as he finished his meal and proceeded to the bathroom to shower. His demeanor reflected irritation. Once Talyn was finished with her food, her mom escorted her to the bathroom to brush her teeth and send her off to bed so that she could tend to Darnell's needs.

Lying back in the tub, Darnell had his head up to the ceiling eyes shut. She undressed and stood there contemplating whether she should join him or not; he looked so relaxed and finally at ease. The answer was simple, her foot slowly eased into their Jacuzzi tub as she attempted not to touch him. Once her second foot landed, he opened his eyes slightly startled. He grabbed her arm and pulled her down onto him. "I miss you," he kissed her lips while she laughed. "So what happened?" Tamia was overly concerned by this point. She sat back against the opposite end of Darnell waiting for the story. He sighed heavily realizing that she wouldn't give it up. "Okay so one of my most effective, main witnesses in the one case I told you about with the guy that was apparently set up by the police. He's on trial for possession of pretty much everything you can think of. Do you remember?"

"Yes, the Williams vs. State case. The really big one I remember," she was surprised and even more anxious now to hear what happened. "The motherfucker gets on the stand and basically retracts his whole testimony!" "Are you serious?" Tamia could not believe her ears. This case was very important for the success of the firm. Although it did not determine the success it definitely would have made a huge difference for them: when a witness retracts their statement that pretty much prolongs the case as well as does not help his client in beating the case. Evidence is pretty much null and void at this point.

"Yes. I'm just as surprised as you are. What makes the situation even worse is that I believe the fucking cop got to him but I can't prove it. Now I'm at a standstill and my client threatening leaving if I don't fix it like I'm the one that got his ass into this mess in the first place. After all the hard work I already put forth in this case you want to fire me." Obviously he had to get it all out. He was fuming. Tamia almost regretted making him bring it up. "Damn, baby I'm so sorry. You'll figure it out I know you will," she attempted to console him. "Have you considered reaching out to one of your connects that can track people's phones?" "I did actually but that'll have to be my last resort because it'll be done under the table and that's always hard to enter into evidence." Darnell was getting even more irritated by the second the longer they talked about it. So, she briefly changed the subject, washed up then headed for bed.

When you're the boss there is no such thing as oversleeping and being late for work, Tamia had to remind herself of that fact after she woke startled of how late in the morning it was; although it was only 9 o'clock. Luckily Starbucks was directly across from her office because after the long conversation she and her husband so deeply fell into the night before - she needed it. If she wasn't trying to accomplish this fashion show sooner than later, she would have stayed in bed a little longer but there was work that needed to get done.

To her surprise, once she entered the office everyone was already busy at work. Demetri made flyers for model casting as well as had Micah advertise it on the internet for the coming weekend. Jarvis was already informed and also recruiting models of his own to rock the runway. Demetri also booked the Landing to have the event. T. Lyric, a local poetic phenomenon, which happened to be an old school mate of Jarvis Rashad, insisted on hosting the event. Both Tamia and Jarvis the same were ecstatic. They knew she'd have the crowd in tune. DJ Dym was one of the hottest female DJ's in Jacksonville at the time therefore it was only right to have her DJ at the event. After briefly explaining to Dyminique about the event she was more than honored to DJ. Tamia felt that her letting everyone off early the day before really worked out in their favor. Within 24 hours everything was already pretty much scheduled and set in stone. All that was left was time.

The potential models were already lined up outside the Chauncey R. Morgan Liberty Center once Demetri and Tamia arrived. Casting call wasn't for another two hours and the line kept getting longer and longer. They were surprised to see so many people actually interested in walking in the fashion show. Unfortunately, we all could guess that half of them may not even have what it takes from body figure to walk and just their all-around demeanor in general. Florida people are always looking for a way to be in the spotlight regardless of whether they can play the part or not. Demetri wanted to walk the line and conduct a pre-interview to shorten it but boss insisted on giving everyone a fair chance. He was just being his normal messy self.

Once they were all set up, the models started rolling in one by one and rolling out by the bunch. Very few fit the requirements, from the way the clothes fit on them, to their own personal look and style, and even worse their walks. Things were starting to look like they were going on a downward spiral. One female approached the table with what appeared to be an "Instagram selfie" printed out on regular printer paper. Demetri bluntly asked her what it was, he felt insulted. Tamia insisted on giving her a chance anyways considering she had a nice figure. "Go ahead and walk to the end of the hall, strike a pose, walk back up, pose again, then exit," Tamia directed. She did as she was told. They could not believe their eyes, she literally started walking like there was something stuck in her ass the way she intentionally sunk it in, turned her toes inward as if she was pigeon-toed and even worse as if it were cute. As if the presentation couldn't get any worse, she posed like a 12-year-old on MySpace with duck lips and a peace sign. Demetri wanted to tell her to continue on her way out after she completed her walk; but as always Tamia sympathized. She stopped him in his tracks the instant he opened his mouth. "I just have one question," Tamia noticed that she did not walk pigeon-ted when she first walked in. "Why would you intentionally walk like that? Even your normal walk is perfectly fine." The poor girl just stood there, distraught. Embarrassed! "Walk again," Tamia wanted to give her another chance. She started walking and without second thought she did it again. They dropped their heads in sync.

"You're a lost cause," Demetri rudely stated, "You can go." Tamia turned towards Demetri, her mouth on the floor, "*Whyyyyy*?"

The girl proceeded towards the exit, humiliated. They could all tell by her demeanor that she was mortified. "Now that was just disgraceful and you know it," Demetri spoke bluntly.

That was just one of many horrendous acts of degradation that occurred that morning. Not sure where these people came from or who told any of them that they were models but based on portfolios and physical appearances these people looked like extras from B.A.P.S. Everything seemed to be going downhill, then suddenly a higher power answered their prayers when Jarvis finally decided to show up with about 16 people: children, men and women whom were already dressed in the gear. They walked for Demetri and Tamia and they were instantly relieved. He showed up and saved the day as well as his fashion show. Along with the few that originally auditioned and actually made the cut, they had approximately 30 models.

They had a brief meeting with the finalists to discuss dress rehearsals as well as all other important matters regarding the event. "This will be a huge event," Tamia exclaimed, "There will be a lot of people in the building, a lot of huge names that many of you may recognize. Females do not act like groupies, and males you don't either. Do not embarrass us and most importantly don't embarrass yourselves. This is an important event considering it represents the introduction to something major for Mr. Rashad as well as all of you. So, if you want to ensure your spot, I suggest you guys eat healthy, don't gain any weight, hit the gym if you need to, just no major changes, ok? If there are any surprises, we will have problems, therefore if something comes up you guys can reach out to myself or Demetri and let him know. Everybody understand?" The group replied in sync, "Understood!" As everyone began to leave the building Jarvis pulled Tamia off to the side to share his gratitude. "I'm just doing my job," she reminded him. "I know; it's just really starting to become real to me." "Don't go getting soft on me Mr. Tough Guy," Tamia was surprised to be hearing these words from the same guy that contemplated for months on end working for her, took two weeks to hit her back, and the same guy that had no interest in fame. Funny how a little motivation and support can sway a person's goals. Jarvis followed her out of the building and over to her car. Trying to be a gentleman he opened the driver's door for her to get in. She stopped for a second and gazed around before thanking him and stepping inside her car. Tamia was always hesitant when it came to men being polite to her. She had a bad habit of being paranoid and mistaking it for flirting rather than generous acts of kindness. Like it was just impossible for an attractive man to be polite to an attractive woman and not expect anything in return. Unfortunately, that is the time that we live in.

"Have a nice day Mr. Rashad," she said as she drove off.

CHAPTER III
Pride Walk

Jarvis

The palms of my hands sweating profusely, my legs won't stop moving, and even worse I keep biting my lips. It was so embarrassing; a guy perceived as hard, unemotional, and nonchalant showing all of the signs of a nervous little girl. But I couldn't help it, as much as I wanted to portray power and strength, unfortunately I couldn't gather those feelings. But today was really the day, my day. The models were looking good, my clothes were looking even better, DJ Dym was doing her things on the ones and twos, and it just couldn't get any better than that. Although, it was only my first fashion show more than anything it was about what it represented for me. Like Tamia said, "It was the beginning of something new, something fresh, life-changing". That was exactly what it felt like for me: life changing. Just to think that I almost passed up this experience of a lifetime. Tamia was really making this happen for me.

"How is everybody doing tonight? Y'all excited for the Pride Walk?" The title came from the name of the brand: Pride and Glory. The crowd went bananas. I couldn't believe they're reaction, and it was all for me. "So, before I introduce the man of the hour, first I'd like to introduce you to Pride and Glory." She went on for approximately 5 minutes glorifying my name as well as my production, and giving the audience background on the line.

"Let me G up, can't let anyone see me like this," I whispered, looking around to see if anyone heard me speaking to myself. Standing behind that curtain listening to all the things T. Lyric was saying about me; I was in awe myself, like who cat is she speaking of? Out of nowhere Tamia ran up to me and asked if I'd seen Tarshay, which happened to be one of my girls. Instantly, I remembered she called me the morning of talking about she was feeling sick. Jaclyn, another one of the models I brought, told me she was pregnant and she knew it. Honestly, I was so overwhelmed I forgot to fill in Tamia and Demetri. I knew she would be upset anyways because the damn girl already knew she was pregnant so why the hell would she even audition. "The fucking girl had morning sickness, talking about she not gone make it," I told Tamia.

"Are you fucking serious?" I had never heard Tamia curse but obviously she was upset, I mean who wouldn't be. "You wait until the last minute to tell us something we should have already known. As a matter of fact, something that we didn't even need to know because she shouldn't have come in the first place talking about she wanted to do the Pride Walk." She had the body and the looks though, I insisted. That baby wasn't showing yet either. "So, she's pregnant?"

Tamia was upset.

"You know what; I don't have time for this shit. Where is Sharaine? They're about the same weight. SHARAINE!" Tamia had to think fast, she wasn't going to allow some random ass female to ruin my show, and quite frankly I wasn't either. That's one thing I admired about Tamia. She was kind and ambitious but fierce when time called for her to be.

I called through my ear piece to inform T. Lyric to continue to speak, stall, improvise, and basically do what she does best: speak free considering we had to make a minor change. Sharaine finally showed up, and after speaking her mind briefly she started getting dressed. Her outfit was a two-piece jumper with a pair of wedges. It must've been God because they were the same size shoes and all. The jump suit fit Raine like a glove. Tamia had to speak some life into her. She was tripping because as nice of a body that she has, she hated to flaunt it. "Girl, you are beautiful and your body is banging. You better get out there and walk that runway. You wanna get paid right?" Tamia jokingly threatened her. It worked, because as soon as she said that Sharaine was dressed within seconds. She fixed her hair up on her own and denied the make-up artists. Sharaine was fine as hell anyways so I'm happy ole girl didn't show. I don't know why she was tripping she should have been one of the models anyways. Finally, everybody was dressed and lined up. I made my way to my seat on the front row closest to the runway. "All ready," Tamia informed T. Lyric.

T. Lyric got the crowd on their feet. Leave it to her to be extra. DJ Dym began the Runway Show playing Big Rings by Drake; the perfect theme song for the event considering the obvious. The entire crowd started screaming and clapping. Once the first models graced the stage with their presence the crowd went bananas. It was a male, a female, and a little girl. Their outfits had the same color scheme as well as similar in format. The little girl wore a denim jump suit with the words PRIDE and GLORY on the front in graffiti, with a pair of classic Shelton Addidas, and a P.A.G backpack with P.A.G. written in graffiti text also. Sharaine wore a fitted two-piece jump suit. Boy did that jump suit do her all the justice. My boy Dontray also wore a denim jumper, with a plaid shirt wrapped around his waist just to add a little swagger, with a pair of Yeezy's. Had to put 3 of the dopest designs on the runway first.

Of course, best for last.

As I gazed through the crowd, my eyes instantly stopped on this sexy young lady: brown skin, long thick curly hair, sitting with her legs crossed and to my surprise Jordan Retro 12s on her feet, with a notepad on her lap. Dayum, who is that? Has to be someone important, she just carried that demeanor. She appeared to be closely analyzing the models and writing at the same time. I'm not sure what she is writing but it better not be any bullshit. The moment I stood and began to walk over to speak to her I noticed it was Shannon Taylor from "Duval Reppin" blog. I don't know why I was surprised to see her here considering she is basically the gossip girl in town. Talking about one single person that knows everything that's going on and everyone's business, she's the woman. I would've invited her if I had thought about it but then again that would have been rhetorical because she's always on every scene. I figured I'd just wait until after the show to see if she'd approach me, I'm sure she'll have some comments and questions to ask.

Focusing my attention back on the stage, it was time for the raffle which represented we were a third of the way in the show. DJ Dym brought the music to a halt and T. Lyric asked the crowd, "Everybody enjoying the show so far?" They all screamed yes. "If I can have everyone take out the tickets they received at the door, we will be doing the first raffle of the night. Y'all like free shit right." I laughed. That girl is crazy; we needed that type of energy for the show. "It'll be a pink ticket, which all my ladies have. The number is 005-36-21." Instantly a young lady in the back of the audience started jumping up and down screaming. You would've thought she won the lotto or something the way she reacted. Security escorted her onto the stage. Demetri walked from behind the curtain with a bag in tow, dressed to impress in his very own nude P.A.G blazer, white V-neck shirt, slacks and Steve Madden slippers. I had to give it to my man; his sweet ass sure knew how to dress. "What's your name baby?" "Bianca!" the winner stated. "Let's see what's in the bag." She put her hands inside the bag and pulled out a huge purple and white letterman jacket with the words Pride and Glory in purple bold italic writing on the back. "This is tight," she put it on her back and left the stage.

"I have to get me one myself," T. Lyric suggested. "Hey Jarvis," she turned towards me on the front row, "make sure I get one of those after the show, you owe me anyways." The crowd laughed. "Now let's get back to it." DJ Dym started the show back up with 'All Eyes on You' by Meek Mill, Nicki Minaj and Chris Brown. I had to give it to her, she made the perfect up to date playlist for the event. From the look of it, the crowd was enjoying the music and most importantly enjoying the show. Next up on roll call was strictly ladies. From classy attire, to casual summer wear the clothes were definitely versatile and targeted for any and every woman. There were clothes for the modest as well as the hoochie's. I think I take more pride in the design of the women's clothes more than the men and children. I know it takes a lot of creativity and talent to be able to make a woman's clothes that their actually interested in.

As picky as women are!

As the show was coming to an end T. Lyric announced the last raffle winner which was for a child. The prize was a black and gold P.A.G. backpack with praying hands on it, similar to the backpack the child wore in the beginning of the runway. The child appeared to be ecstatic. That moment alone did something powerful to me. I felt a chill going down my spine. The kids were my motivation for the line in the first place. Directly after the raffle, she presented the Kinesthetic Kids to the stage. The Kinesthetic Kids are a group of young dancers from this Artistic School over on the south side. These youngsters can definitely put on a show. They had the crowd on their feet, dancing, clapping and screaming the entire performance.

Once I realized it was time for the last group I swiftly but smoothly ran to the backstage. I put on my blazer, changed my shoes to a pair of loafers that Tamia damn near begged me to wear. Talking about I needed to show versatility in my attire as a clothing designer. I proceeded to the dressing room, grabbed my special guest and escorted her to the runway. All of the models just stopped and stared in admiration. I walked her over to the curtain and on queue she did her thing. My 63-year-old mom worked that stage like no other. I knew Mama Dell would come through for her son. I had to create a special outfit for her. She was dressed in a long black hi-low blazer with the logo on the lower front pocket, a blue blouse underneath, black Capri slacks, and to my surprise some heels. I don't remember moms wearing heels since, I don't remember at all. Once she reached the end of the walk-way she took her jacket off then turned around presented the back of the blouse to the crowd. It had the word Pride big, bold and glittery at the top of the blouse, Glory big, bold and glittery at the bottom of the blouse and the logo in the middle in the form of rhinestones. It was the first time I had tried the pattern and the crowd seemed to love it. Photographers were snapping left and right and my mom was soaking it all up. I couldn't help but laugh. "You are something else," I turned around and it was Tamia. "It was only right," I told her. I walked out of the curtain and met my mother on the cat walk. We walked down to the end together and I gave my lasting speech. I wrote something to say but then again I figured it was a little cliché' so I decided to come off the dome with it. I looked around the crowd slowly, analyzing and appreciating every face in view as I could see the admiration in their body language. It took me a second to get my words out; my mother could feel the apprehension so she rubbed my back. Mothers always know don't they.

"Just speak from the heart," she said. So, I did just that. I spoke from a place of gratitude. Even if nothing more came about after this event, it was enough to make me feel like I accomplished a lifetime's worth of success bearing in mind my background. I ended with, "I appreciate all of you for coming out, and I really hope you enjoyed the show. Even if you don't like the product for yourself, all I ask is that you respect the hustle of a little 12-year-old that couldn't see his life going any further than a life in the streets but had the strength and the will to overcome that stigma. I owe it all to God and this lady right here," I said as I hugged my mom. "I want to give one last shout out to a woman that remained persistent with me and helped make all of this happen, Tamia!" The crowd gave a warm standing ovation as Tamia walked onto the stage. She without a doubt worked the stage like a natural. The three of us held hands, bowed then exited the stage. DJ Dym kept the music playing for the meet and greet portion of the event.

I had several people approaching me from every angle trying to get pictures as well as ask me questions. I slick felt like a celebrity. Honestly, I didn't have time for that shit though, I never understood why famous people would duck and dodge these people but if it is anything like this then I can imagine how rough that might be. I had my sights set on Ms. Shannon Taylor. I'm sure she planned to find me but quite frankly I'm not a patient man so I figured I'd look for her myself. I was pacing the room dodging the paparazzi's left and right and yet she was nowhere to be found. I didn't want to make it too obvious but she was nowhere on the main deck. As I continued to look for her, I ran into one of my exes Ja'lyssa. The last person I expected to see here. Immediately I turned away and she grabbed my arm. "Not here yo," I told her sternly and attempted to walk away again.

"I just wanna congratulate you," she claimed. I knew she was lying. "Thank you," I said then started walking.

"Can we talk?"

"Look Lyssa, I'm not talking to you here and I'm not talking to you now," I didn't want to be rude but I just couldn't believe she was brave enough to show up here. The main bitch that said I wasn't going to be shit, tried to convince me to be a dealer like my father knowing where that got him and had the audacity to say this clothing line would go nowhere, shows up to my fashion show being thirsty. Oh, the irony, right? This was not the place and it definitely wasn't the time. Just as I was soaking up the moment, the devil had to roll up and bring in the negativity to balance it out. I damn near had security escort her out but I didn't want to resort to that so once again I attempted to be the bigger person and walk away. Just as I did, right there in plain view stood Shannon. It must've been God answering my prayers because I needed something to really get me away from this girl before I flip out. I knew if she saw me talking to another female that she'd do one of two things. Either she's going to get jealous and leave or get jealous and act a fool. I figured it was worth me taking my chances.

There she stood, watching my every move as I motioned towards her just guiding me in her direction with her eyes. I felt seduced even though I was the one that planned to do the seducing. "Wassup? Did you enjoy the show?" "It was entertaining and organized well," she stated. "Anything you saw that you like?" Shannon totally ignored my question and preceded with her own, "So, what exactly led you to start this line in the first place?" "You answer my question I'll answer yours," I joking gave her an ultimatum. Before she even had a chance to respond Ja'lyssa decided to intervene. I was so lost in a daze by finally running into Shannon Taylor I didn't even verify if she had left. I should've known this crazy ass girl would resort with option 2 of 2.

"Is this your new bitch?" She asked with her hand on her hip and her body positioned between the two of us. The fucking nerve of this broad was foreseen, but I didn't necessarily believe that she would brave enough to actually confront us. Before Shannon even had a chance to respond I grabbed Lyssa by the arm and dragged her ass toward the exit. At that point all I could think about was the ball that I know a blogger would have with that situation. That situation definitely escalated for no reason at all. Drama, supposed baby mama's, wanna-be homies, and family are known to step out of the wood works when they believe someone is about to be famous or already are. I had no tolerance for that shit especially at my first event. Hopefully Shannon understands that much and reconsiders going wild on my name in her blog.

Once we reached the exit door, I motioned for Security to kick her out and not allow her to come back in. When I arrived at the location that Shannon and I previously stood before being rudely interrupted by Lyssa, she was no longer there. FUCK! I knew there would be no point in trying to find her after a story like that. Bloggers live for shit like that. I didn't know if I should reach out to her and attempt to talk her out of it or just allow nature to take its course. She may not even write on it, and then again who am I fooling if it was me I would. After standing there contemplating for a moment, I found myself daydreaming. Once I awoke T. Lyric was standing there in my face, just staring. She damn near scared the shit out of me with the poker face she was holding on to. "Damn girl," we both laughed.

"So, about that Letterman though?" I see she wasn't going to give it up. So, I escorted her back stage and showed her a few different styles that we had readily available. "Those are all nice but can I get my own designed with T. Lyric on the front?" "You already getting it free, you want me to make you your own and customize it. What do you think this is girl, Burger King?" Although, low-key it was a serious question I said it in a joking manner. "Thanks love. When will it be ready?" She just knew I'd do it for her. It was the least I could do after paying her for hosting the show, also right? No, wrong!

The meet and greet was coming to an end and people were starting to exit. The event was a great turn out and surprisingly I was able to get rid of all of the products I brought for show as well as gain a new list of clientele. After a long successful afternoon, I was ready to get these damn loafers off of my feet and go to sleep. Realizing I hadn't seen Tamia since we were all on stage I went backstage to see if she was still back there. Like I assumed she was back there with Demetri, Sharaine and Lisa directing the cleaning crew. Demetri, Sharaine and Lisa waved to us and left. Demetri had a little smirk on his face as if he knew something we didn't. "How does it feel?" Tamia asked. "Man, life never felt so good. My dreams are coming true. Who would've thought?" Maybe I was getting a little ahead of myself but for me that was more dreaming than any dreaming I'd ever done. "That's good Mr. Rashad. I'm so happy for you," she said trying to be formal. I used to let that Mr. Rashad shit slide but it actually annoys the hell out of me. For a minute I confused me allowing her to call me that for turning me on rather simply not trying to be impolite.

"Call me Jarvis please," I asked her, "we've been working together long enough now for you to quit that Mr. Rashad bull." "Sorry Jarvis." She said with a smile surprised at his request.

"Oh, before I forget," I said to her as I quickly walked away to grab a bag that I had hidden before the show. "I want you to have this and know how thankful I am for remaining consistent with me, I never had anyone believe in me like you did from jump and honestly I didn't know how to take it; whether you were being funny or scheming. But now I see you had good intentions for me. I know this business is going to go far for me now." "No worries, it's my job, Jarvis." She reminded me. She continued to stand there, smiling at me. I moved closer toward her admiring the crinkle in her eye that I noticed she gets every time she smiled. I couldn't help but to crack a smile myself. We both just stood there speechless, it was awkward at first. Instantly I felt something, I knew she wanted me, I knew she wanted it. Wasn't sure whether I should run with it or leave it at that and go on my way. Of course, being the person that I am I took advantage of the situation.

I leaned all the way in towards her and kissed her directly on her soft, desirable red lips.

CHAPTER IV
Denial

Did that really just happen? Did I *really* just cheat on my husband? I sat outside of my house stuck, flabbergasted by his actions. Oddly I still had butterflies in my stomach. I still felt all of the emotions I felt at the exact moment it took place.

My mind knew it was wrong but my body allowed it to happen. It was 8 o'clock at night and my husband knew the Pride Walk would be over by 6 and I still wasn't in the house. I wonder if he knows I'm sitting outside right now. I'm surprised he hasn't hit me up yet questioning my whereabouts. Then again why would he, we had a good relationship, we trusted one another. Maybe I was just being paranoid, but should I tell Darnell what happened? He'd want to know. I'd want to know if I was him. I put my shoes on my feet and got out of the car. Standing at the door, staring at the door with my keys in my right and my left hand on my forehead, I stood there for a short second and contemplated my last question and decided against telling him. We were in a really good place; I refused to be the one to ruin it. I inserted the keys into the door and before I fully unlocked the door, there Talyn was opening the door for me.

"Hey mama's baby," I picked her up, kissed her, and placed her back on the floor. I was happy to see my baby, today felt longer than usual. Just that quick I forgot he put his lips on me and I just kissed my baby. I was instantly disgusted with myself, I was just ready to shower, have a glass of wine and go to sleep. Darnell was there sitting on the couch watching the basketball game. He turned around right away once I grabbed a hold of his shoulders. I kissed him on the cheek then started to my bedroom. I already knew I wasn't going to get away with it, my husband knew me better than anyone and never have I arrived home kissed him on the cheek for one, not say a word two and head straight for my bedroom. It was formula for accusation and I couldn't blame him if he decided to question me about it. Then again, I'd be offended if he didn't. I started a bubble bath, undressed and stepped into the bathtub. The water was scorching hot, almost burned the skin right off of my bones. I guess I wasn't paying attention, my mind was elsewhere. I couldn't wait to wash away the sin so I stepped into the tub anyways without waiting for it to cool. It was really hot but I ignored the temperature and lied back on my bath pillow.

It felt as if I had been laying there for at least an hour once I finally opened my eyes to the sound of Darnell's voice asking, "Baby are you okay?"

"Yes love, I'm fine just had a long day. I'm tired." I tried my best to play down my true feelings. I laid my head back down and closed my eyes. "Don't fall asleep in there. I'll be waiting for you." He turned away from me, left out and closed the bathroom door although I had left it open anyways. I couldn't pinpoint it exactly, he wasn't being himself either or maybe he was just concerned. I sped up my bath, took a quick shower and stepped out of the tub. I threw my robe on and got in the bed as I was. Most cases where an individual would get caught cheating was because they had a hard time sticking to their normal routine. Typically, I would put on lotion, my panties and pajamas, and tie my hair up unless I had something else in mind that called for no clothes at all. But just like others that would get caught cheating, I altered my routine also; unintentionally, of course. I turned my lamp off on my side of the bed and attempted to go to sleep facing the wall. Darnell grabbed me by my shoulder and turned me over towards him.

"Yes boo?" I responded to his aggressive gesture. He just sat there and stared into my eyes, squinting as if trying to figure me out. "Boo I'm tired." Trying to get him to say what was on his mind so I could go to sleep. "How was it," he asked?

"How was what?"

"Huh, the Pride Walk." I'm sure I puzzled the shit out of him with that paranoid ass response.

"Ooohh, it was a good turnout. A lot of people showed up and they enjoyed it. I ended up having to stay longer because the owner wanted us to stay until the cleaning crew finished ensuring cleanliness or we could've been charged for destruction." "Oh okay, that would've sucked. You couldn't get your assistants to stay?" he asked out of curiosity considering my position. "I mean I could have but you know what they say, if you want something done right do it yourself. At the end of the day the money would have come out of my pocket so I figured I'd just stay to be sure the money would stay in my pocket you know." We both briefly tickled by my statement.

"I understand. What about this Jarvis guy?" I rebutted quickly, "What about him?" As soon as I responded with those words and the tone that I vocalized I wanted to retract that statement as soon as possible. It was as if I had an out of body experience because I could hear myself and see my facial expression in response to his question and how wrong it might've come off. I instantly attempted to answer what I presumed he could have been asking, "He loved it. You should've been there; he brought his mother out on the runway and all. The crowd went bananas. He was able to get rid of a lot of his products and gain a lot of clientele too."

Darnell was aware of what I was trying to do and allowed it to pass. I could tell since he hesitated before responding. My eyes were beginning to close involuntarily; I tried my best to keep them open so it wouldn't come off rude as if I was trying to go to sleep on him while he was talking. I hated when people would do it to me so I didn't want to be a hypocrite but I was really tired and it was starting to show. "Go ahead, you can go to sleep. You look finished" "I am babe." I turned over and went to sleep.

When I woke up in the morning, I was feeling relieved and refreshed. It was a nice day outside, my husband had breakfast ready for once and Talyn was up and out with some school mates. "Someone woke up on the right side of the bed this morning?" I asked him considering the nice gesture. It either had to be my birthday or Valentine's Day in order to get my husband to step into the kitchen for me. I refused to question the occasion and just accepted it for what it was. He took the tray off of my lap, placed it on my night stand and kissed me. His lips were so luscious and soft; I instantly fell into his trap as always and grabbed his head pulling him closer towards me. He slowly began to peel my robe off of me as he continuously kissed me all over my face. I already knew what was next. "I have to go to work," I wined as I pretended to turn away from him as if I didn't want all he had to offer.

"Come on baby, just 10 minutes I promise you won't be late." Without hesitation he rubbed my clitoris and without a doubt I was sold. "I swear to you if you make me late, I know something." I threatened him. He ignored everything I said and right away he went to work. As he inserted his dick inside of me disregarding the pain, I was bound to feel taking into account he was not his usual gentle self. "Damn baby," I squealed as I slapped him on top of his head. "Girl, calm down, don't fight it." If I wasn't as paranoid as I was the night before I'd assume, I was being punished for something I was not aware of. He pounded me for all of 10 minutes. He was moving in and out of me quickly as if he were doing a high intensity interval workout. I stared into his eyes as he began to cum inside of me. I loved the faces he would make as he came; it was as if he saw the light or something. I felt so accomplished every time. I grabbed him by his ass cheeks and pulled him inside of me until I could feel every inch of him inside of my body. "What are you trying to do make a baby?" he asked me.

"Are you going to give me one this time?" I asked him inquiring. He ignored my statement and just fell on top of me and rested his head on my shoulder. "I told you I have to go to work," I attempted to roll him over off of me so I could get up and get dressed for work. "Move boy," I repeated. He was stronger than me. He laughed at my failure to get him off of me and rolled over. I took a quick shower, got dressed and left for work.

Luckily, I had no one to answer to regarding my punctuality. But after the day I had yesterday I needed that much. Even when I got to work, Demetri had already begun drafting ideas with Sharaine in regards to the new calendar of events for the following month for Jarvis. Honestly, I didn't even want to speak his name or think of him, but there was work that needed to be done and I knew better than to allow my personal life to affect the professional environment. I just hoped he knew how to do the same. Once I walked in my office, my eyes instantly gravitated towards the balloons, flowers and gift on my desk. Immediately I assumed it was my husband with his typical 'just because' gestures. Ahhh he's the sweetest, I said to myself as I inhaled the sweet smell of tulips. Darnell knew I loved tulips. I slowly crept around my desk creating suspense hesitant to open the gift seeing as how I love surprises.

"Hurry up!" I turned away frightened at the sound of Demetri and Sharaine's voice as they were being nosy wanting to see what I received also. The fucked up part about it was they knew who it was from and I'm pretty sure my response to it confused them just as much as it confused me. There I was excited yet clueless about whatever it was in the box until I laid eyes on the backpack and just like that my expression changed from delighted and anxious to bothered and angry instantly. "What does it say," Demetri asked before I even had a chance to realize there was a letter there.

"Business," I told him implying he needed to mind his own! I picked up the letter and it stated, "Thanks again Tamia. Thought your daughter might like this." Although, the letter was sweet and harmless for some reason I felt even more bothered by him giving my daughter a gift in the name of lust. I didn't plan to punish her because I knew she would love it; it was pink, purple, gold, and glittery. But the balloons and flowers on the other hand were not called for. It baffled me that he purchased me tulips. How he knew I like tulips, I thought to myself. I knew it would be inappropriate of me to accept the flowers and balloons and just leave them hanging around in my office knowing his intent. I popped the balloons, threw them away along with the flowers. Maybe it was rude, but it was even ruder of him to give them to me knowing I have a husband.

I sat on the edge of my desk and decided I'd go ahead and check my voice messages that had been piling up for the last week or so. The first few messages weren't pertinent but by the 5th message I was in for a surprise. "Really Tam, what's up with the site? Has Micah finished up the layout yet? If I don't hear back from you by the end of this week, we're going to have problems young lady?" It was Keegan and Derrick; two of my most loyal customers since I first opened Her Image. I can remember the day I met them as if it were yesterday. Two goofy ass jocks walking into my business, I just knew they were lost. They just started looking around and totally disregarded me standing there observing there every move. They even had the nerve to hold a conversation regarding the appearance of my business. Once they finally conjured up the ability to speak to me the first things, they said to me of all things, in sync was -

"*Hey, you work out?*"

All I could think was really, really do I work out. Where I grew up two white men walking into your place of business of that stature were asking for trouble. Being the new-found business woman that I was I knew I had to remain professional so in a joking manner I replied, "Can't you tell?" "We damn sure can, that's why I asked?" Keegan responded. He had this really raspy voice, I almost thought he was hoarse until I met with him again and realized it was his normal voice.

"Well thank you," I replied, "Now how can I help

you." Derrick took the lead and in a very narcissistic tone he stated, "Seeing as though we pretty much own this area and realized it was new business in our neighborhood, we figured we'd check you out. So, what do you do?" Although I was somewhat offended and every bone in my body prevented me from replying with, *"Well if this was as much of your neighborhood as you claim it is wouldn't you know what I do here?"* But instead I kept it simple, explained my business and from that moment forward I gained two goofy ass loyal customers who surprisingly respected what I do and loved spending money with me. They owned a gym in the area and they had me market everything for them; flyers for their events, social media posts and my current project that I seemed to have failed them were the website that Micah was working on.

"Micah," I yelled into his workspace and summoned him into my office. "Wassup boss," he asked. I played the voice message for him and gave him a chance to answer before I interrogated him. "Oh shit!" "Before you say anything I know it's not your fault considering we've been so busy with other things but where are you at with the website so I can call these nuts and let them know the status of it." "I'll get on it and finish it as soon as possible. I pretty much have the," I interrupted mid-talk and insisted that he left and got to it. "Let me know when you're done."

The rest of the voice messages consisted of messages from other clients, potential clients from the fashion show, and my annoying daughter who loves to just call and play on my phone. I figured the least I could do was call back some of those potential clients. I was never one to allow money to slip by. As I was in the middle of a phone call, Demetri beeped in with Jarvis on the line. "Take a message and tell him I'll get back with him later." Before I even had a chance to continue my conversation Demetri was beeping in again to inform me that what Jarvis wanted was apparently important which I doubted. "Tell him I'll call him right back, I promise." Demetri's tone sounded just as confused as mine did regarding the fact that I just left my client hanging in the wind like I did. But I was in the middle of business just as I can assume that what he wanted had nothing to do with business. Or at least I'd like to hope it did. And to my surprise I was right; Jarvis didn't want a damn thing. He was only calling to confirm receipt of his gift. I was getting frustrated by the minute hearing his voice but I maintained my composure. "I am in the middle of a business call right now Mr. Rashad so if there isn't anything else, I will get back to you at my earliest convenience." I stated, waited for confirmation that he didn't want anything else and hung up the line.

I sat back in to my seat, annoyed and bothered. I

couldn't believe I was allowing this little boy to get me so hot like he was. I refused to allow it to continue. To get my mind off of things in the meantime I decided to make my rounds in the back where all of the physical work was occurring between Lisa, Sharaine, Micah and a few new employees I just recently hired to assist with their workload. Just as I could expect, they were just as surprised as I was to see me within their territory. I trusted them and never felt the need to watch over them at work but today was different. Plus, I was bored. "You guys hungry, can I get you guys anything for lunch I'm thinking Pinera Bread?" Sharaine walked over to where I was and placed her palm over my forehead. "Rain what are you doing?" I asked her confused although I understood the sarcasm. "You sure you aren't sick?" They all laughed. "Ha, ha, ha very funny," I replied as I walked around observing the work that was taking place. "What brings you to the hood?" Micah was the funny man on campus. He always called their work area the hood because he claimed that I was too classy to come back there. This is true enough as I stated earlier, I don't come back here much. But I'm sure if I visited more often than I do then they wouldn't like that very much either.

"Are you guys hungry or not?" I ignored him as I took everyone else's orders and exited the premises.

As if my day couldn't get any better or worse, when I pulled back into my parking spot after retrieving my hoodlums some food in my peripheral, I could see that red and black Lexus pull into the parking lot. You would've thought he hopped out of his car and ran as fast as he made it to me. "Let me help you with that." He grabbed the bags out of my hands without even allowing me to affirm or deny. "No thank you, I got it." I grabbed the bags out of his hands and proceeded towards the door. I knew by now he should have been able to tell I had some sort of animosity towards him after our last encounter.

"At least allow me to open the door for you," he opened the door and waited for me to walk inside. I stopped in mid-transit and just looked at him. I rolled my eyes being childish and continued towards my destination. "Hey Jarvis," Demetri greeted him in his usual flirtatious tone as he waved his spirit fingers in the air. Jarvis was used to it by now and compared to when they first met, he was much more comfortable with his flirtatious mannerisms. He said Demetri was actually a cool dude, surprisingly; and it no longer bothered him.

"What up De?" he responded as if they were close friends. Jarvis escorted me as I took the hoodlums their food. "Oh, this is where you guys hide out?" Clients don't typically come back here but seeing as how Jarvis took it upon himself to join me, he was able to see their personal work center. I figured right, as soon as we entered the space together, they all looked at us with googly eyes as if something were going on between the two of us. I shook my head disagreeing as I handed them all their food. "Get back to work," I told them in a semi-arrogant tone jokingly and left. As I was closing the door, I could overhear the childish chatter and laughter regarding both of us coming back there. Although, it was a coincidence that the two of us just happened to pull up to my business at the same time I knew they would think we were together and start with the rumors. I wasn't sure if I should dead it right there or not. Then again that would probably confirm their accusations if they had any to begin with. Maybe I was over thinking it.

Let me just get back to work so I can get my mind off of this nonsense.

Jarvis went out of his way yet again to jump in front of me once I attempted to make entry into my office to open the door for me. "You can stop with all that extra stuff," I told him. I had enough of him making a scene in public. It was inappropriate and I'm sure if anyone saw it, they'd agree as well as assume I didn't mind. "Damn, a man just can't open the door for a woman out of respect. My bad," Jarvis was highly offended and you could see it all over his face. But did I give a damn? Definitely did not, I wanted him to understand there was nothing there and no need for the "gentleman" like gestures. He could save it for someone that was interested. I sat down at my desk and immediately changed my demeanor and addressed my client. "Anyway, what can I do for you today Mr. Rashad?" He just sat there and stared at me rubbing his chin as if I was speaking another language or something. I pushed my neck out and gestured for him to speak.

"Really it's like that Mia?" Then he had the nerve to call me by the nickname only my husband and friends called me. "Don't call me that," I said while shaking my head. "But what's up what do you need?" I tried to get him to move on with it. "Why you acting funny?" he asked me as if he didn't recall how he invaded my space and tried me a few nights ago. "Are you seriously asking me that? Look Jarvis we are not about to talk about this right now, and especially not in my place of business. So, if it's not about business then you serve no purpose here right now." I gave it to him as straight as I could. Might have sounded rude, but I was already getting funny looks from my people so I just wanted to kill it as best I could before it escalated. He just sat there, looking puzzled and dumbfounded. Out of nowhere he just started nodding his head and smirking as if he had something up his sleeve. "It's like that," he asked? "Cool, cool!" He got up from his seat, headed for the door and before he walked out, he turned around looked toward me, shook his head then slammed my door. You would have thought I had just broken up with him the way he reacted. I really didn't want this to affect our working relationship but from the way he reacted I was sure it had. My mind was playing games with me but I wasn't about to allow this foolishness to fuck with my head and affect my work. Nothing a little drink wouldn't cure.

I figured there was no greater person to help me relieve my minor stress and take a break away from work than Salina. Although she was at work I figured since she was interning with my husband that I'd be able to pull her away from work for a good hour or two. Unfortunately, I thought wrong. After somewhat expressing my feelings to Salina briefly and requesting her presence at Friday's for a quick bite to eat and a drink on me, to my surprise she denied. Apparently, she was busy working, assisting picking up the pieces from Darnell's previous case with the witness that changed its story. Even though I wanted to phone Darnell and beg him to give her a break, I reconsidered. There was no point in me taking her away from work when she obviously wanted to be there; or had to.

I wasn't ready to give up my request for some girl time so I dialed Tonya's line. Luckily it was around her break time anyways, and being the smart woman, she was she refused to turn down a free meal. Once I arrived at the restaurant, I ordered two waters and a glass of white wine just to get me by until Tonya arrived. Tonya was taking forever and Friday's was actually closer to her than it was to my job. As I waited, I had no choice but to sit there and rethink what happened with Jarvis earlier this morning. *Maybe I was overreacting*, I thought. *There was no point in ruining our working relationship over something as petty as the situation was. I don't even think I gave him a chance to see if he could remain professional with the exception of his demeanor. But I'm sure I pushed him to respond in the fashion that he chose.* I pulled my phone out of my clutch and decided to give him a call, apologize and possibly set up a meeting the following week to talk about ideas for the future. But before I even had a chance to locate his number in my phone considering I had deleted the contact, Tonya snuck up behind me and hugged my neck. "Hey boo, I've missed you." I stated as I kissed her cheek. "Sit!" I directed for her to take a seat and join me at the bar. "What's going on with you," she asked? "I had a long morning, I just needed to get out of the office for a while you know. What about you? How's life?" Even though I invited her out to eat so I could share with her current events I knew it was only right I asked taking into account her relationship status. Boy did I bite off more than I could chew with that question. I already had a few cups of wine in my system when Tonya arrived and hearing her ramble on about Rodney was not a part of the plan. I knew it would be rude for me to interrupt her while she was talking but I just couldn't take anymore.

"You and that darn Rodney. You just can't get enough of that man, can you?" I asked her as I smoothly interrupted her in the middle of telling me her whole life story as if I didn't already know. "Sad but true," she admitted. "Girl, you will not believe it..." The liquor almost enticed me to tell her everything. But then I remembered who I was talking to and decided against doing that. It probably wasn't smart for me to tell Tonya that I had been working with a young man that is attracted to me and now I'm stuck between losing him as a client just in case this situation gets worse. Although, I did not want to risk that I didn't want to put my marriage at risk either. I knew if I had told Tonya about Jarvis, she would be judgmental considering she admired me and Darnell's marriage. So, I had to think quickly on my feet and make up some additional news.

"What is it?" She asked excitedly. Her reaction reinforced my original thought process so I picked up my cup of wine, took another sip and proceeded with my news. "Darnell and I are going to renew our vows and I would like for you to be my maid of honor," I told her smiling as hard as I could. Her face appeared to be even more excited than I was for something that I immediately realized would have to come to pass because I knew Tonya would stay on me about it.

Tonya placed both of her hands over her mouth and from the look on her face she appeared to be getting emotional. "Really, I am more than honored Tam." She hugged my neck as tight as she could until I could barely take in air.

Okay okay girl, I get it you're happy. You're starting to choke me," I said while laughing and untying her arms from around my neck at the same time. I'm sure the main reason Tonya was so excited was because she was upset about not being my maid of honor when I initially got married. Needless to say, I should have considering me and my original maid of honor, Jacqueline, were no longer friends. I don't know what the hell came over me and provoked me to say that we were renewing our vows of all things. I had bit off more than I could chew with that statement. The waitress had finally returned to our table. I didn't even realize it had been so long since she last checked on us because we were busy talking. "What can I get you guys today?" "I'm not even hungry anymore," she was gone so long I had lost my appetite. Tonya looked over at me in awe surprised that I would ask her out to eat and not even eat.

"What about you ma'am," she referred to Tonya? "Yes, lady I'll take an appetizer, since someone doesn't want to eat anymore. Wings and blue cheese please." The waitress wrote her order down, left our table immediately as if she were in a rush. "She's definitely going to earn her tip," I told Tonya sarcastically. "Don't be rude now Tam," Tonya of all the friends swore she was the mom. She treated us all like the little sisters she never had. We finished up our conversation with a host of ideas that Tonya suddenly contracted during our brief outing regarding the reception. The waitress returned with our checks and did not say a word. I presume she knew she was in the wrong. Just as I promised I wrote a 0 on the check for gratuity and departed. I looked at the time and noticed it was getting late and I decided instead of going back to work I'd just go straight home. I called Demetri and informed him of my plans and just told him to take care of everything else and lock up.

I arrived home to an empty house, it was so quiet I could hear the minute hand on the clock ticking away, 'tick tock, tick tock'. Talyn was at the after-school program and Darnell was still at work. I would have gone back to work myself but after the morning I had endured I needed some alone time especially considering that I did not to effectively utilize my girl time. I plopped down on the sofa and turned the television to my favorite station, lifetime. "One More Chance" was playing yet again for the third night in a row. I couldn't stand to watch that movie one more time. As I passed through the channels, I sadly realized there was nothing good playing on the television so I decided to grab my kindle and read a book. Before I could even turn the page, I shortly realized that I was not focused and had not a clue of what I had just read. My head was definitely elsewhere. Maybe I should just give him a call, I thought and quickly argued against that. I knew damn well that was a bad idea but for some reason I felt we really needed to have that talk or else I would have lost a valued client – one that I worked so hard to book. No point in allowing my stubbornness to get the better of me. It never had before; not since I was a child anyways, and today was not going to mark the start of a new bad habit. After I took a shower, I threw myself onto my bed just as I was, bare skin and cool air and before I knew it, I was woken up with a soft whisper in my ear. I didn't even realize I fell asleep. "What time is it," I asked him? "10:30."

"Dammit," I hopped up instantly not thinking to just ask Darnell. I couldn't believe I had been sleep for so long. I ran around my room like a race horse searching for my purse and something to throw on. "What's wrong baby?" Darnell asked clueless and concerned. "Where is Talyn?" I continued on my quest. "Baby calm down, I picked her up," Darnell assured me of her safety. I sighed deeply, relieved yet disappointed. "You must've been tired, it's okay baby." I couldn't even muster any words to say. Today was my day to pick her up from school considering Darnell had been working late the past few weeks dealing with this case and I just left my sweet child hanging. My husband understood but being tired was no excuse and I didn't want to allow it to justify my neglect. "How long was she waiting do you know." "Tam she's fine, don't stress yourself over nothing." I suddenly felt comforted and at ease as his lips gently pressed against my forehead. He kissed me on my cheek, then my other cheek, he lifted my face as I began to pucker my lips then he kissed me on my chin. I opened my eyes to see him staring into mine then unexpectedly he licked my face.

"Eew, why would you do that," I asked while slapping him across the head jokingly. "Damn girl, did you have to slap me though?" "Maybe not but you deserved it, had me so worried for no reason." "Hey you were the one that forgot," he laughed as if it was funny. My facial expression instantly changed, "That was a low blow. Where is my baby anyways?" "It was a joke, don't be sensitive. She's in her room sleep; she ate and took a bath now you just relax." "Check you out being a nurturing father!" I smirked. We were both on a roll but it was all love at the end of the day. Plus, I was only speaking a fact. Darnell almost always left it up to me to handle specific tasks, and Talyn being the main of all those tasks. I could barely pay the man to cook, help Talyn with her homework; nothing more than work, watching his sports and criminal shows. Typical.

I threw my robe and slippers on so that I could go

check on Talyn. She was sound asleep, cuddled up like a baby holding so tightly to her build a bear her dad purchased her for Valentine's Day. I kissed her softly on the cheek, cut her night light off and left her room. I arrived back in our room to an obviously horny man who was ass naked sitting up in the bed as if he just knew I was coming back ready for it. Unfortunately, although I was already dressed for the occasion or shall I say not so dressed, I just wasn't in the mood. I was exhausted more so mentally than physically. I totally disregarded what I knew was expected, kissed him goodnight and turned over to go to sleep. I could feel his eyes piercing through the back of my skull as I lied facing away from him. He kissed me on my neck, grabbed me by the waist and pulled me closer to him. I could tell by his aggressiveness what he was attempting to do. I turned over quickly and just gave him the eye, then attempted to go to sleep again. Before I could even give him a chance to seduce me, I told him that I wasn't in the mood. I knew that 'No' was not an answer that Darnell took often nor kindly. Not saying that he would force himself on me but he was spoiled just as I was and we were both to blame. To my surprise he let me be. The bed rocked suddenly; I turned around to see Darnell leaving the room. I assumed he was going to the living room to watch TV or something.

Every time he would get upset with me, before I even had a chance to consider putting him on the couch, he put himself there ironically. Generally, he would just take a few hours until he cooled off or I was asleep then come back to bed. By that time, I would be over it anyways. I liked to test how well I knew my husband so I went to the living room and peeked around the corner and just as I suspected, he was laying on the couch watching TV. He saw me peeking and gestured for me to come over. I turned the other way as if to go back into the room, "Mia, come here please." I walked back into the living room and lied down on his lap; it wasn't before long that I was knocked out cold.

When I woke the next morning, Darnell was already gone to work and I assume he took Talyn to school also. I looked at the time and it was still early. I must've just missed him. I turned on the Bluetooth on my phone and connected to my portable speaker. Music was the one thing that helped me to get my mind right for work every morning. I pulled out my clothes to iron them as I danced around like a little child. My shuffle always seemed to play the right music at the right time. *'I get so weak in the knees I could hardly speak...'* as soon as I heard those lyrics blast through the speaker I was instantly distracted. I grabbed the closest thing that resembled a microphone which happened to be the Glade air freshener, and pretended to be at a concert lip singing one of my favorite tunes. That song brought back so many memories. My most fond memory which ironically wasn't quite a good memory for Darnell was when he and I were in high school. We were still, as my dad would call it, courting at the time and he took me out on a date to a drive through movie. We were too busy talking and getting to know one another, we barely gave the movie the time of day. He was rambling on about his basketball games of course and the music was playing low in the background adding a soundtrack to our story time. As soon as I heard those lyrics, without hesitation I interrupted him to sing "Weak" by SWV. I blasted the song through the roof. I'm sure everyone could hear me in their cars since I was singing louder than the music. Darnell just stared at me smirking and I'm positive it wasn't because I had a nice voice. It was as if he wasn't even sitting there, I was in my own world until suddenly; BOOM! His speakers blew. I didn't know what the hell happened but his expression displayed enough information for me to conclude it wasn't anything good. He just looked forward with this poker face that just appeared to be unbreakable. I tried my best to console him because I could tell he was very upset. Surprisingly this 17-year-old young man handled his anger very well, better than I expected, and after about 6 minutes of complete silence he looked over at this confused little girl and said, "It's cool girl, I liked your voice better anyways." I laughed and leaned in to kiss him.

It was the perfect moment for us to share our first kiss which also became our first time. Well my first time. Although I trust my husband, till this day I still find it very hard to believe that he was a virgin at the time. I mean he was just too good and from my perception, experienced to be a virgin. We made love that night, to the tune of "Weak" in my head and the sweet sound of lust coming from my mouth serenading him every second of it. Just as I was about to reach my climax there was a bright light flashing through and a sudden tap at the window. Scaring the living crap out of me, like seriously I damn near shit my pants. Darnell didn't even roll his window down to see who it was; he just started his car and pulled off. As the guy attempted to chase us down, we zoomed off into the wind laughing up a storm. So, every time I hear that song, I can't help but recall a night to remember. On the other hand, whenever Darnell would hear it, he'd remind me that I owe him a pair of speakers. Even still till this day.

I arrived to work that morning with a long list of meetings that Demetri set up for me today. Unfortunately, Jarvis was on that list for 1030. I'm sure Demetri squeezed him in because I did not recall receiving a reminder the day before. As much as I didn't want to potentially encounter a repeat of our last meeting, I had to get that thought out of my mind and think strictly business. I stuck to my normal routine prior to my first meeting, which was with Keegan and Derrick. I checked my emails, voicemails, updated my calendar, and lastly prepared the documents for my upcoming meetings. I called for Micah into my office so that I could be sure that he had his presentation ready for the Cross fit twins to view. "All set, I'm reviewing it right now," he assured me. "Be sure to have it set up in the conference room prior to their arrival. I want to get straight to the point so they can be in and out." "Got it your highness," Micah smirked at me. "Shut up boy," I couldn't help but laugh. As much as I can't stand that fool and he irks my nerves, all of them, you just got to love him. Always keep you laughing.

Demetri rung my line to inform me they had arrived. They were a little earlier than expected, but I didn't mind, the sooner they came the sooner they leave. Demetri escorted them into the conference room. When Micah and I walked in they had already welcomed themselves to the condiments. "Well, well, well look what we have here," Derrick greeted me in his usual sarcastic, flirtatious tone. Derrick had an undercover thing for black women. I'm sure he doesn't think I know but I have always caught him watching me but not just that, he went on a date with Sharaine. But you would never be able to tell, he keeps it on the low. "I see you guys have already welcomed yourselves to the condiments, you're welcome." "Well they were for us right," Keegan asked. That raspy voice of his will definitely take some getting used to, and I'm positive I'll never get used to it. "Sure, why not?" I answered sarcastically, "Now can we get to the business of this meeting please." I walked around the table in front of the screen. I resumed with my duties and went over the documentation that outlined the website. Derrick and Keegan appeared to like what they were hearing considering they would look at each other constantly and nod in sync. Those guys were definitely created for one another; anyone would be surprised to discover that they weren't related.

"Can we just see the website already," Keegan asked. I know that I've failed them lately considering I had been so busy with Jarvis, but I wasn't going to take much more of his sarcasm. I gestured to Micah to go ahead and start the presentation. He allowed the video to play for a few seconds before he began narrating through it. As he finished, the cross-fit twins started whispering back and forth in one another's ears. Micah and I looked at one another confused and patiently awaited their opinions. They continued to whisper. "Do you guys just insist on always being so rude?" I was growing impatient and agitated with their gestures.

"Well," and before he had a chance to finish speaking, I already knew it was going to be something, "the presentation was nice." "What did you like sir and what could I change to make it better," Micah could be professional when the environment called for it. Derrick and Keegan went on for at least 5 minutes explaining more of what could be changed than what they actually liked about the website. Micah took notes as they spoke so he could make the changes accordingly. Honestly, I believed the presentation was just as good as the website. Derrick and Keegan just wanted to live up to their names as assholes and to add we have been somewhat neglecting them lately. "Derrick. Seriously," I asked? I had grown frustrated the longer he spoke. "Micah has worked really hard on this website and did it to the best of his abilities according to your request. I know you're upset with me right now but that's for us to work out. Don't take it out on him and make him redo the entire website." Derrick and Keegan just stared at me. I'm quite sure that they were astonished by my blunt and straight forwardness but I knew what it was. Not only that, they had an insurance policy to have their website redone if they did not approve of it within 15 days of putting it online. This was another method for us to get out of abiding by that considering I never assumed we'd need to.

Derrick stated, "You're right." "Now what," Keegan put his hands up in a rude manner, "Going to make the corrections *or not?*"

I instantly grew mad but quickly regained my composure and professionalism, "Yes we will, is there anything else we can do for you two?" At this point I was just ready for them to go. "Have it done by the end of the week." "Of course, sir, I'll start on the corrections right now." Micah stated as he left the conference room. He was just as frustrated as I was and that was the easiest way for him to get away. I gestured for them to leave, "Have a good day fellas." They proceeded to leave and as Derrick held the door for Keegan to walk through, he had to stop and add something. "Look, I like you Tamia. Just don't forget about us again okay." Keegan stated as he opened his arms gesturing for a hug. I had t0 exert all willpower towards being generous and hugging him after all of the bull crap they had just given us regarding the website. I gave a brief smirk smile and kissed both of his cheeks. Their Italian, you know how that go.

As soon as the door closed, I turned around and just stared at Demetri with a look of relief as I rolled my eyes. "Don't let them stress you boss," Demetri was surprised that I even allowed them to get to me. "I'm fine. They were just being assholes and giving Micah a hard time." "Forget them now. You have your next meeting coming up with Jarvis soon." I could always count on Demetri to keep me sane. Although, I never told him anything regarding what happened with us, I knew he could tell that Jarvis had been driving me crazy lately.

I walked back into my office, plopped down in my comfy chair and just massaged my temple. I had to mentally prepare myself to meet with Jarvis; after all we left off on a bad note. I rang in to the front desk to ensure that Demetri had everything ready for my next meeting. Before I could fully hang the phone up and sit back in my chair Demetri was walking in with the paperwork. I looked over everything one last time to be sure everything I planned to go over was there and of course it was.

Demetri escorted Jarvis to Tamia's office. Jarvis appeared to be a little uneasy considering his facial expression. He walked in and sat down directly in front of me just staring in my eyes, looking right through me. I ignored the awkwardness and continued with our meeting, "How are you doing Mr. Rashad?" "I'm good, you alright?" "I'm fine." I began placing the documents in front of him as I explained them one by one. Although he appeared to be inattentive, I continued to explain. Once I got to the Calendar, I needed to ensure that he was paying attention, "So we have a host of events, well ideas that we would like to do for PAG. Look over the Calendar if you will and let me know what you think. The next thing I would like to do is try to set up a meeting with a few popular hosts, radio personalities, DJs, etc about having them wear your clothes during some big events. What do you think?" Jarvis just continued to stare at her, he hadn't said one word besides 'I'm good, you alright' since he had walked into her office. He sat back in the seat, relaxed with his arms out along the arms of the chair just staring. He really had a bad habit of just staring and not saying a word. It was starting to feel more and more awkward. His request for a meeting was not work related at all; we'd covered that much so far. He wanted to speak on our last encounter I presume. I didn't, there was no need to.

"That's cool with me," he stated in a monotone voice. It was as if he didn't care regardless. I could've told him that I wanted to set up a meeting with a local cleaning service to use his clothes as rags and his salty behind would have agreed to it. "Are you sure you're good?" I looked at him out the corner of my eye with a mere smirk attempting to lighten the mood. I honestly didn't care to know but he was making it really difficult for me to discuss business with him. "I just don't understand you." He looked at me confused, as if trying to read me. I've always took pride in being unreadable and people have a hard time dealing with that. Except for Darnell of course, he didn't allow me to intimidate him and that's how we've gotten this far now. "Look, you really want to do this right now. Can we please just move on and act like nothing happened. I'm really trying to help you here. I want you to be successful. I need you to be successful. You have a real talent and you deserve to go far. Let's not allow some simple mistake to interfere with our business relationship because I really can't deal with this." Jarvis was surprised.

"A mistake?" he asked astounded.

"Yes, a mistake. You caught me off guard." I replied, confused. He spoke as if I intentionally lead him on. "Word!? I caught you off guard. You were asking for it." "Don't insult me or my marriage. We are not about to do this right now. Listen, it happened, it's over, get over it."

Jarvis got up from the chair.

"Call me when you're not in denial then we can get back to business."

I could not believe what I was hearing. I stood up from my chair and gestured for Jarvis to sit back down. "Sit your ass down. Don't you dare come in my office with that bull shit? Okay, I get it. It happened, well really you did it. I allowed it, I fucked up. It's nothing there, I'm married and Darnell isn't going anywhere. It was in the heat of the moment, now what's next? What do you want from me? I'm trying to help you make more of yourself and you just want to keep shitting on me for the sake of your ego. No! I will not continue to kiss your ass, I have enough clients and I make enough money, and I will continue to make even more money and accrue even more clients after you. So, if you want to continue this we can, if not take our contract, shred it and don't come back to my office. Yes, it's that serious," as I threw my hands up. I couldn't believe I had allowed this young man to disturb my humble nature and snap the way I did. But I was not going to allow him to come at me as if I needed him. Jarvis instantly brightened his mood. You could see it in his eyes. He slowly moved back towards the chair and started looking over everything. Maybe I was tripping, but I would have thought they he liked what he was hearing the way he was smiling to himself. I was lost for a second as I continued to stand and await his response. He eventually looked up from the calendar and asked, "Is that how you feel?"

"Yes, now what is it going to be?" I crossed my arms across my chest. I needed him to understand that I meant business. "I understand Ms. Tamia," he smirked. I could tell he had something up his sleeve, but I didn't want to think that far.

"Now back to business or what?" "I'll take this stuff, look over it and let you know if there are any changes." He stated as he grasped a hold of all of the documents and placed them in his backpack. "Be easy." He walked out of my office.

Once I completed my last meeting with Alex Racoda I texted Salina in need of her upbeat and entertaining presence. It had been a few weeks since I had a chance to hang out with my girl. Even though she annoys the hell out of me sometimes she was still one of my best friends. Before driving off I called Darnell to let him know I'd be home a little later since I was going to Salina's house. He obviously was missing me considering he questioned why but I don't ask him questions when he hangs out with the boys so that was irrelevant. She still hadn't text me back and since she wasn't at work, I figured she must've been home, or possibly out 'hoeing' knowing her.

'Knock, knock.... Knock.' No answer. The lights were on inside, so I knocked again. She had to be inside or else why would she have left her lights on. She had a garage so I couldn't tell if she was in or not. She would only leave her car out if she wasn't in for the night. I waited a few more seconds then decided to locate her extra key inside the flower pot that we all did alike in the case of emergencies. I crept inside slowly attempting not to make too much noise just in case she may have been sleeping. The den was clear, living room clear, kitchen clear, so I proceeded towards her bedroom. When I got to the entrance of her bedroom, I couldn't believe my eyes. It felt as if something unexpectedly yanked me by my bun the way my neck transited to the rear in shock. I knew my friend was a little promiscuous but I never thought she'd go to an all-time low. I stood there briefly stuck unable to move with a look of disgust on my face. Surprisingly they didn't even notice I was there. I at least would have felt the presence of someone watching me but I presume they were both too caught up in the moment. He was standing leaned up against the wall with his head down and eyes closed as if to be praying. While holding on to Salina's waist, she was bent over face down ass up letting him pound her rapidly. Then suddenly, the guy looked up and as soon as I saw that baby face I knew exactly who he was: the fucking kid from the restaurant the last time we went out to eat. *What was his name? Uuum, Michel or something like that.* As soon as he saw me, he stopped and threw his hands up in shock as if they had just gotten caught by her mother. Salina looked back at him confused then noticed his facial expression and turned to look in my direction.

"What the fuck Tam!?" she unattached herself from him then ran after to me as I headed towards the exit. I covered my eyes while attempting to grab a hold of the door knob and look away from her naked body. "Girl my bad I didn't mean to interrupt your little baby making session with a baby. I'll see you later." I turned back towards the door and attempted to twist the knob. She grabbed my shoulder firmly and turned me around. "No, what are you doing here anyways?" "Girl, never mind it. This may be a surprise to you but no one wants to talk to you while you're naked. I'll see you later nasty."

She yelled hey to get my attention then said, "Oh yeah by the way, *I told you he wanted me!*"

CHAPTER V

Transgression

The skies were clear and blue; the sun was shining bright, and the sound of chatter and kids' laughing set the tone. It was the perfect day for a play date at the park with Tonya's children. Since Talyn was the only child they would have random play dates so that she could have some children her age to play with. Once upon a time Rodney would come also and him and Darnell would end up leaving Tam and Tonya with the kids while they went to the pool hall. It had been a while since Darnell and Rodney saw one another, "Hey Tonya, how has my dude Rodney been lately. You talk to him?" Ironically, he already knew about their relationship, but it was a very sensitive topic and she didn't especially want everyone to know about them still messing around. But who didn't know that they were still messing around? Anyone that knew Tonya personally as well as Rodney knew those two couldn't stay away from one another. They couldn't live with one another and can't live without one another.

"He's fine I guess." She stated as if she didn't know the actual answer. Her eyes cut left as if to check how Tam was looking. They were best friends of course she knew that they were still kicking it, and she was Darnell's wife and best friend so you know she tells him everything.

Rodney Jr. interrupted them in the middle of talking by running over and throwing the ball at Darnell. Darnell caught the ball and took off running with it while leaving the women to their gossip thing. Rodney Jr. looked just like his father; Big Rod couldn't deny him even if he wanted too. Darnell once wanted a son himself but turns out his beautiful baby girl ended up being more than enough. Plus, he ended up with two godsons, Jr and Roderick; they kept his hands full enough to satisfy his once desire. He ran over to the court and threw the ball to Roderick so he could have it since his older brother always teased him. Talyn was busy swinging with Rody while the other kids ran around them playing tag. Tamia loved to watch Darnell interact with the kids, he was really good with them. She wanted more but they hadn't been so fortunate to get pregnant lately.

"Sooooo," Tonya whispered to Tam as if someone could possibly be listening to them, "*have you guys started planning for the vow renewal wedding?*" Tam hadn't even said anything to Darnell about it yet and honestly, she had forgotten. Seems Tonya was more focused on it than Tam was which means that Tam had to get with the program or else tell the truth. This was not going to happen seeing how Tam took a lot of pride in the appearance of their marriage. She did her best at keeping her friends at an arms distance when it came to their personal relationship. Tam knew better – Tonya's relationship or lack thereof reminded Tam all the time the damage keeping your friends in your business would do. "I think we're just going to do a reception with our close friends and immediate family, nothing too extravagant." Extravagant happened to be in Tamia's nature so that statement alone had taken Tonya for a loop. "That's unlike you, why not do it big. This is a big moment for you two. Married almost 5 years, now right?" Tamia smiled blissfully, that was a huge accomplishment in her family. "Yes almost 5. But there's no point in wasting unnecessary money just to renew our vows, we did it up for the wedding enough for a lifetime." She reminded her laughing. "Speaking of, remember how you started crying when you walked in to the arena?" The ladies shared a laugh.

Tamia briefly reminisced on that day; she still couldn't believe it herself. She typically wasn't the most sensitive, especially not in public but that day she couldn't hold back her tears…

Tamia's old best friend Jacqueline had hired a wedding planner out of Tampa, Sunny Aslot was her name. Sunny was The Wedding Planner. All Jacqueline had to do was say two words: "Do you." And, that's exactly what Sunny did. Jacqueline and

Sunny asked Tamia in unison as all of the other bridesmaids stood behind her anxious, "Are you ready? "As soon as Tamia replied 'of course', two very handsome men opened the doors and before Tamia could even take two full steps inside, she instantly stopped and gasped for air as if she had seen her worst nightmare.

"Go ahead," Jacqueline declared as she gave her a little nudge, "look!"

Tamia looked left then looked right and straight ahead again and instantly started tearing up. You would have thought something was wrong with her but it was the good cry, tears of joy. Jacqueline grabbed her hand and guided her further inside to get a better look. She couldn't believe her eyes, it was everything she had dreamed of and more. The chairs were all covered in nude seat covers with teal bows hanging off of the back of them. They were aligned in the shape of a V so that everyone could get a good look at them as they walked down the aisle. Tamia looked down smirked and looked back at Sunny. Teal was her favorite color, but Sunny had really overdone it with the teal carpet. In a good manner though. There were instruments to the right and in front of the right side of the chairs as if there would be a live band. Tamia's heart dropped into her stomach upon realization of what the sight of instruments meant. She loved live music and to think she'd have a live band at her wedding, that excited her. "Who's performing?" she asked.

"It's a surprise," Jacqueline stated. Tamia continued slowly walking through the arena as the rest of her friends ventured off on their own tour. She walked up under the canopy where they'd be saying their vows and gracefully rubbed her hands across the flowers that were enwrapping it. She loved tulips and they were dyed to match the wedding theme also. The soft smooth texture of the petals as she softly touched the tulips aroused her even more. She didn't even give herself a chance to finish touring the arena before she broke down crying, this moment was so surreal to her. The sight of their pictures in the slideshow that was on the big screen hanging from the ceiling added to her sensitivity. The girls ran over to Tamia as the sniffling grabbed their attention. On the other hand Salina was too busy flirting with one of the men that opened the door when they entered to even realize.

"Girl are you okay, you should be excited," Tonya asked her? "It's just so beautiful," she cried out.

Tonya and Tamia both laughed at the thought alone. "It's just so beautiful," Tonya mocked Tam pretending to cry holding her head down with her hands over her eyes. The accuracy left Tamia embarrassed. "Leave me alone!" "Did you ever tell

Darnell about this?" She continued laughing. Darnell rejoined them in the middle of their conversation and instantly Tamia became nervous. She started to bite the inside of her lip. "Ouch!"

"What's wrong baby?" Darnell asked concerned and confused considering he did not visually see anything hurt her. "I bit the inside of my lip," she giggled as she grabbed her mouth. Tonya and Darnell briefly looked at one another then shared a laugh. It appeared Tamia only did that to distract them after the conversation he'd interrupted. Talk about awkward, she hadn't even had a chance to tell him herself. Good thing that did the job. "Tonya, how's the clinic been?"
"Fine," she said, "I can't complain too much it's a job after all."

The children kept playing until they were short of breath. Talyn ran over to her mother, Rody in tow and placed herself on her lap. They wiped the girls down then prepared their bags to leave. "Boys, time to go!" Tonya screamed towards the basketball court. Little Rod and Roderick continued to play. Tonya got onto her feet and walked towards the basketball court yelling, "Boys, I said its time to go." They whipped their heads around looking dispirited. "But mom, we're not done playing." She walked over to Little Rod and yanked him by his ears dragging him towards the car. Roderick followed in suit. "Bye, I'll see you guys later," Tonya called towards Darnell and Tamia as she headed towards the parking lot.

The sun was just starting to go down once they arrived home. Tamia immediately got Talyn ready for bed then attended to her husband. She didn't have a plan as to how she would go about asking Darnell to renew their vows so she figured, oh well, just go for it. She waltzes into the bedroom, he was there waiting for her sitting alongside the bed. He grabbed her by the waist, picked her up and rolled her over on top of him. He could feel the temptation in her hazel eyes radiate through his soul when she looked into his eyes. He wanted her just as much as she wanted him. She took her index finger and traced the outline of his lips. He loved when she did that, it turned him on even more. She felt his penis instantly poke her as he started lightly humping her like a pulse. She continued to tease him while contemplating if it was the perfect moment to bring it to his attention. The print of his hard dick against her vagina made her want to rip his pants off but she insisted- she insisted that instead she should just get to the point and get it over with before sex became a deciding factor.

He placed his fingers up against her lips stopping her from speaking as she whispered 'but babe' to him. Pretty sure he wasn't trying to hear anything that was coming out of her mouth if they weren't moans or anything similar to directing him to give it to her. He looked at her confused as she peeled off top of him. Tamia didn't typically make a habit of denying him sex but she had a good reason this time. She grabbed a hold of his hands, caressing them as she pulled them closer to her. Darnell could not believe that she had stopped him right before he was about to give it all to her plus more. He had gone all day, the past few days without fucking his wife and he had enough of it. "Can I just say something," she asked attempting to soothe his frustration with her tone and fluttering her eyelashes, "I promise you, afterwards it's all yours." She managed to crack a smirk out of him.

He fixed his posture from bothered and frustrated to attentive and alert prepared to hear whatever was so important she had to interrupt. "So, I was thinking," she was hesitant, unsure exactly how to say it. You would have thought she was asking him to marry her as if they hadn't already surpassed the hard part. "Since we are coming up on our 5-year anniversary, what better way to celebrate it than renewing our vows?" Confused, speechless, he was unable to utter a word. He was baffled. Then he realized her facial expression had slowly changed considering he was making her feel awkward like he was going to say no. "You mean to tell me you took all the time in the world to speak just to ask me to renew our vows again." "Uuum, what's the problem?" She appeared just as confused as he was but for a different reason. "Girl I will marry you every day until I'm on my death bed then right before I finally lay to rest, I'll marry you again," he instantly buttered her up while laughing at himself. Darnell always knew all of the right things to say to constantly sweep his wife off her feet. It was words like that, which allowed him to win her over in the first place.

"Ahhh baby," she kissed him in on his lips several times, "I love you." "It's mine now right," he expeditiously changed the subject ready to get back to his original business. He stroked her upper thigh with his fingers gesturing for her to take her panties off. She did exactly as she was directed then we know what took place next.

"De why are you always knocking on the door, come on in," she yelled to the door after she heard persistent knocking assuming it was Demetri. They still refused to come in. "Come in, I'm not moving from my chair." The delivery man walked into the office and placed the Edible Arrangements and a letter on her desk. "I'm sorry about that," she said feeling slightly bad for her laziness. "Thank you so much." She didn't waste any time devouring her fruit before opening the letter. She opened the card and in it was written, *before I marry you again girl, I need you to get yourself together lol. I love you boo.* Darnell had sent her on an all-inclusive spa retreat plus one to Miami Beach. "This man is too much," she told herself blushing. She texted his phone multiple smiley faces thanking him for his kind gesture.

The trip was within the next two weeks so she didn't waste any more time inviting Tonya and planning a shopping trip for the two of them before their departure. At first Tonya was a little undecided; she didn't think that she'd be able to get 4 days off work on a two-week notice. But it was already taken care of so she couldn't refuse.

Tamia, Tonya and Salina met up at the Avenues Mall to do a little shopping. They stopped in the food court to grab a quick bite to eat before leaving. "So, what's been going on with you heffas lately," Salina asked. "Now the question is what's been going on with you and your new little boyfriend, pervert," Salina laughed although Tamia was serious while Tonya just sat there looking lost and confused. "Little boyfriend?" Tonya looked at Tamia then at Salina awaiting an explanation. "I know you don't have a child." "Don't look so disgusted Tonya damn." Salina and Tonya could never get through a full sitting without arguing. "Anyways Tamia, since your nosey ass wanna know," Salina turned in her seat facing away from Tonya, "Michel called me after all." "Who is Michel?" Tonya asked. "I'm pretty sure I wasn't talking to you." "Stop being so damn childish, y'all two act like caddy ass teenage girls." They both just stop and look at Tamia surprised that she was cursing like that. "What? Don't look at me like that now anyways what were...." Tonya interrupted them yet again, "Who is Michel." She was itching to know. "The boy from the

Cheesecake factory the last time we went out to eat," Tamia told her to shut her up already so she could learn how this transpired, "Remember?"

"Talking about the young boy that she was flirting with the whole time and left her number with?" Tonya asked. "Yes damn," Salina was getting irritated by the second. "Like I was saying he ended up calling me after all. He was just a little shy and embarrassed at the restaurant that's all that was. But I told you he wanted me."
"I get it, why do you have to keep saying that. Still doesn't make it right." "Girl he's 23." "You saying that like you not pushing 30," Tonya laughed. Salina finished sharing with them how great his sex was and how she was actually considering making him her boyfriend despite the fact that he was younger than her.

"So, are you going to miss us when we're gone?" Tonya asked Salina. Tamia's eyes instantly pierced Tonya's skull as soon as she asked her that. She quickly attempted to retract her question but it was too late, she had already done the damage. Tamia hadn't told her where they were going because she knew Salina would be upset and jealous because she wasn't invited. But Salina knew just as well as Tamia and Darnell that she didn't make for good company on a trip as such. Salina was a good friend -at times- but she was also bad news when it came to men and temptation and even worse peer pressure. Her recent relations proved that enough to be true.

"Where are you hoes going?" Salina asked, now curious. "What did I tell you about calling me out of my name?" "Where are y'all going?" Salina rolls her eyes. "Darnell is sending us on a spa retreat to Miami Beach as a wedding anniversary present next week."

"And I'm not invited?"

"I only got a plus one and don't make me say why you weren't my plus one." Salina insisted on knowing why anyways so like the blunt person that Tamia was she straight up told her why. Salina was well aware of her flaws and promiscuous ways. They finished their meal briefly and headed home. Salina was pretty upset about not being able to go with them. She figured the least, they could've told her and she could have bought her own ticket but quite frankly they didn't want her to go.

When Salina arrived home her future boyfriend Michel was there waiting for her, on the couch, legs spread eagle but naked like he lived there. She was in awe that he was even bold enough to be there laid up like that waiting for her arrival. All she could think is what if she arrived home with one of her other boos. Lord knows how that would have turned out. She had left him there in the bed asleep when she left out this morning assuming that he would eventually get up and go to work or something. Not lie around and wait for her to come home. Salina was fuming with discomfort. But who could she blame? Why would you leave him there, alone, anyways? She was already upset about not being invited to Miami Beach so instead she took it out on Michel. He just sat there, confused, unaware about what he was soon in far. Salina kindly and humbly asked him to get dressed and leave. He stood up walked closer to her and wrapped his arms around her waist yanking her closer to him. She pushed him a little too hard and just like that his reflexes enticed him to smack her open handed. Salina was light-skinned too so her face instantly bruised and turned red. She held onto her cheek, her eyes widened, the pain was slowly increasing; she couldn't believe he had just put his hands on her. Realizing what he had done, he quickly walked to her room to get dressed and leave. Salina was in shock, she had never experienced domestic violence, and she didn't know what to do. As much as she wanted to attack him, she couldn't gather enough energy or courage to do so. He slammed the door as he walked out and she didn't plan to see him again.

Tamia woke bright, early and bushy tailed Monday morning so they could get a head start to the airport for their flight to Miami Beach. Filled with excitement, she brewed her favorite blueberry coffee and blasted her speaker while she finished getting dressed. Her phone rang interrupting her dancing session- it was Tonya calling inquiring an approximate time she would be picked up to go. Darnell was still asleep and she wanted to wait for him to wake up before she decided to wake him up herself and go. He was sleeping so well, cuddled up like a baby she really didn't want to wake him. Her flight was scheduled to leave in the next two hours and they lived at least 20 minutes away. Darnell woke appearing groggy and bothered and immediately Tamia felt bad, "Sorry baby I'm getting ready to head out."

The cold in his eyes was restricting his vision as he tried to see clearly. He rubbed his fingertips in the crease of his eyes as Tamia kissed him on his lips. "Baby wake up, I'm about to leave." She kissed him again. "Alright boo, have fun. I'll see you when you get back." He returned back to the fetal position and attempted to go back to sleep. To no avail- so he decided to just go ahead and get ready for work.

Darnell arrived to work so early; his employees weren't even in yet. Before he could get fully settled in Salina texted him saying that she wouldn't make it to work today. He wasn't going to just let that fly without an explanation. She tried to blame it on cramping but Darnell knew better, he had a wife; it was *nothing a Motrin couldn't help,* he thought. He had a feeling it was something else but he just let it fly, this once.

After a 2-hour flight, Tonya and Tamia had finally arrived to Miami Beach. They were excited. It had been a while since Tamia had gone on a trip since she opened up Her Image and it had been even longer since Tonya went on one. Tonya planned to enjoy herself considering she barely got time away from her children. Well, she never had time away from her children besides her being at work or them at school. Miami Beach was not ready for these two. Although their trip consisted of several benefits to include their actual spa scheduled on the second day, they planned to make good use of the other 3 days they were there.

The hotel looked like something Tonya hadn't ever seen before bearing in mind she never stepped foot outside of Jacksonville. Felt as if she had landed overseas somewhere. Her Steve Madden flats graced the concrete, her eyes up to the rooftop, music blazing in her ear drums; she reached out her arms pulling in the fresh air. Butterflies were fluttering in her stomach. Tonya hadn't felt this great in I don't know, years maybe a decade or so. They approached the receptionist with delightful smiles and inquiring minds. After retrieving the keys, they didn't waste any time running up to the suite while their bags were being escorted by the doormen. Everyone was so sweet there, that alone added to their impression of the city. Made her really think she was somewhere foreign especially considering most people from Florida were just outright rude. Totally took away from the stereotype of Southern hospitality or maybe it was just everyone she happened to come in contact with. They loved what they saw the moment they stepped foot inside the door; there was a kitchen to the left, the living room was straight ahead with a big screen TV mounted on the wall welcoming them to their room and granting them a happy stay, their rooms were on both sides of the suite and had bathrooms in each room with entrances from the living room also. It looked like an apartment. Settling in as if they were home, they hung up their clothes, placed their toiletry items on the bathroom countertop, aligned their shoes in front of the bed and they were only expecting to be there a few days. Both Tonya and Tamia put on Maxi dresses, flats, shades and sun hats and set out on their adventure for the day.

Darnell

Tamia must've been enjoying her trip, I hadn't heard from her since they landed Saturday morning. I was going to hit her up and check on her but I figured she was enjoying herself so I just let her be. Salina was still trying to be off work even after I gave her the whole weekend off for her cramping, but I needed her so I made her come back to work. This particular morning her face was caked with makeup and I wouldn't have typically asked about it but it was pretty obvious she was trying to cover something up since I've never noticed her wear makeup. I called her into my office just to check on her and make sure she was better.

"What's up?" she asked like I was bothering her. Once again, obvious something was wrong. "Take a seat." Salina sat down directly in front of him. She couldn't even look him in his eyes. She had purposely put a lot of makeup on that morning because her face was still bruised. Salina was light-skinned too so it wasn't easy for her to hide impurities. "Everything alright with you?"
"Yes I'm fine, why do you ask?" She appeared uncomfortable based on her posture and tone. I didn't want to make her feel any worse but she wasn't making it easy for me either. "I'm just checking on you, making sure you good. We missed you around the office this weekend. Are you feeling better though?" I attempted to show her a bit of sympathy and concern to beguile her to tell me what was going on with her.

She stood up from her seat and headed towards the door. "Yeah I'm fine; let me get back to work a lot of catching up to do." "You're telling me." I laughed, but she didn't crack a smile. I knew something was up with her; she wasn't her usual goofy self. We were used to Salina talking our heads off in the office, roaming around bothering everyone (in a good manner of course), and being outspoken and witty. I didn't like it.

"Salina, sit back down." I directed her in an aggressive tone. She stopped in her tracks- she was definitely shocked, but shit she shocked me with all that damn make up on this morning. I didn't want to be direct and address the makeup so once again I tried to get her to just tell me. "I'm going to ask you this one more time." She was nervous and anxious; she kept playing with her fingers. "What's going on with you? You should have known I was going to know something was up, you don't ever come to work like this," yet again, trying my best to be indirect.

She didn't say anything, she just stared at me. "So, who hit you?" There it was! She took too long to respond. Her mouth instantly dropped and her eyes were glossy. She must've forgotten that I was married to a woman and I have a daughter. I notice everything. She shocked the hell out of me yet again; I didn't expect her to start crying. "Damn, is it that bad? How can you expect me to help you if you don't tell me what's going on? I can't let you just mope around the office like this or let you go if I don't know what's up?"

She could barely catch her breath and speak. When people hyperventilate while crying makes me think their fucking dying, that shit scared me. I walked around the table to console her. Talk about water works! I locked my door, I didn't want my assistant to be all in Salina's business nor get the wrong idea. I was starting to feel bad for her, and thought I'd just let her go home. Obviously, it was a sensitive issue and she didn't want to talk to me about it. I grabbed her tissue off of the table and placed them in her hand. She hugged my neck tight and I returned it briefly but she wouldn't let go. I almost cracked a laugh because she reminded me of Talyn but I didn't want to make her think I was laughing at her. I slowly grabbed her arms and unattached them from around my neck, she was there a little too long. "Salina, you are too beautiful to be letting some nigga put his hands on you. How long has this been going on?" "It hasn't, that's the point." She struggled to stay still trying to catch her breath. My shoulder was drenched in tears and I don't even want to imagine what else. "Damn girl, you're getting snot all on my suit and shit." "Forget your suit, it's probably cheap anyways," she laughed, wiped her face and my shoulder. I didn't bother responding to that comment because we both knew that was a lie anyways. She was finally feeling better and I was glad I could help. I returned to my seat on the other side of my desk.

"You okay now, or do I need to give you the day off to get yourself together?" She just sat there and blushed at me, oddly making me uncomfortable. I couldn't tell what she was thinking; I had a hard time reading her. Honestly, I've always had a hard time reading her.

"Can I ask you something?"

I had no idea what she was going to ask me. Every time someone starts with asking if they can ask you something forewarned you to prepare yourself for some off the wall shit. But I kept my cool and responded, "What is it?" She wiped her face one last time and discarded the dirty tissue. "Did you not think it was awkward for me to work here?" It figures- she probably wanted to ask me that for a while. "What do you mean?" "I'm saying with our history and everything, you don't think it's awkward?"

"Is it awkward for you?" I knew I couldn't get myself out of that one. I wanted dreadfully to get out of having that conversation, but I mean she was right; I knew she'd want to ask eventually. Honestly, I hadn't thought about it. Tamia and I were in a good place and I figured Salina would be over it. Obviously, I was wrong.

"I mean you know I've always wanted you and then after we-" I didn't allow her to finish her statement before I added, "I just wanted to help you out that's all." "You mean to tell me you never thought about what could've been?" She leaned her head over to the side and gave me this confused inquiring look. "Salina." I was stuck; I didn't know what to say. Even though I knew this conversation would come up eventually I didn't think about it nor did I prepare myself for it. 'What to say?' I thought. I just sat there with my hand on my face, rubbing my chin with my fingers.

She started to linger me in, seducing me with her eyes. I dreaded this day, this moment, this second when I'd have to contemplate temptation and doing the right thing. Her eyes were like drugs, get one hint of them and they were addicting. I looked away from her and then felt a soft touch against my ear. I was surprised she still remembered that was one of my spots. It always turned me on a little when a woman would play with my ears. As soon as I turned around, she kissed me on my lips and at the point there was no going back. She took her leg and placed it over mine as she sat on my lap. "You know this is wrong." I told her, "We shouldn't." "But we should," she said, "and it's so right. You know I've been waiting for this moment." She smiles, sadly, desperately begging for pleasure.

She grabbed a hold of my desk and gripped it firmly as she pulled herself up on top of it, legs spread wide and just like that she threw in the bait and reeled me in. It was clean shaven, pink and smelled of something sweet, I couldn't identify the smell but I knew I liked it and wanted it planted on my face. "Are you going to just stare at it, or are you going to taste it," she whispers in my ear softly demeaning me.

I slide my fingers slowly up her thigh, caressing her- her legs quivered at my sudden touch. As my fingers eased into her pussy I felt her vagina walls quench as if she hadn't been penetrated in a while. "Is this what you've been wanting?"

"Yes," she cries out as her eyes roll in the back of her head while leaning back in sync. I was working myself up to get ready so I could finally have her. She quickly grabbed my wrist as if I was hurting her as I rotated my fingers in her. But she just wanted me to stop, "It's my turn."

She slowly unbuttoned her blouse while staring at me with those serenading green eyes. I pinched the zipper on her skirt, and dragged it down until I fully exposed her. Her nipples glistened like pearls; it was something about nipple rings that did something to me. I wanted to suck on them, so that's exactly what I did. She cupped her breasts and massaged them. Her moans were like a lullaby. I removed her hands and took possession of her nipples into my mouth as I sucked them like a pacifier. I twirled her ring around in my mouth then pulled it slightly with my teeth. She looked at me like she was surprised about what that felt like. But I could tell she thought it felt good. I pulled at it again, and again and suddenly she had enough. "I want you inside me," she said. "I want to feel you, stop teasing me."

She hopped off of the table onto my lap and started to undress me piece by piece starting with my blazer. She took off my tie then wrapped it around her neck as an accessory to her already naked body. Once she saw my chiseled chest she stood up and just looked at me with eyes of lust. She grazed her tongue across her lips and started touching herself. I just sat there lost in a daze, I never had someone do that right in front of me but I liked it. It turned me on even more. She licked her fingers then instantly inserted them into her pussy rotating them in and out as she moaned loudly pleasuring herself. She was having too much fun alone so I figured I'd join her. As I began unbuttoning my trousers, she immediately stopped me, "No, let me do it." I stopped after the first button and left the rest for her to proceed. She unzipped my trousers slowly while grazing her hand across my print and at the same time looking me in my eyes reassuring what was about to happen. As much as I hated to admit it, I had been waiting for this moment for a while after our history.

Salina just wanted to do all the work while allowing me to just sit there and be pleasured, and that's exactly what I intended to do- relax and let her take control as she requested. Her knees met with the floor while her hands and tongue met with my dick. The sound of her soaking her mouth preparing herself to receive it all aroused me- and by that time he was more than awake also. She slowly wrapped her mouth around me, and went so deep until I could feel the tip touch the back of her throat. Although a little awkward at first, it was captivating. "Damn," I groaned uncontrollably. It was dripping wet; I could feel it against my leg. Without delay after taking it out of her mouth, she gripped my shaft tightly like a baseball bat and gave me the massage of a lifetime. The feeling was incomparable, unbearable, stimulating. I gripped the bottom of the chair for support as my body started to stroke the inside of her mouth on its own. I couldn't hold it in any longer; she apprehended every ounce of pride I had left in my body. Trying my best to hold it in, my body started to stiffen, my knees started to break stance, and my toes began to cringe inside my Stacey Adams. "Ahhh," it was too late, I was overtaken by sexual hunger and as much as I tried not to let go, he was on his own accord. Opening my eyes embarrassed while attempting to sit up and move her away from me. "Damn!" in awe since she still hadn't stopped. Her mouth is overflowing with cum as she continues to suck me. I watch her as I struggled to keep my cool, then she looked up at me. Overwhelmed, my heart pounding inside my chest, I looked away ashamed- ashamed at the fact that I was enjoying it. It was everything! I was no longer in control of my actions; she had overpowered me and seized all control. The instant my back met with the back of the chair trying to slouch and get even more comfortable there was a knock at the door.

Paranoia took over, but yet the nerves took me over and caused me to be stuck in the moment. There it was again. 'Knock, Knock, Knock.... Knock' it was relentless; they wouldn't stop even though after the first set of knocks no one opened the door. "Boss you sleep in there?" the voice yelled out. *Oh shit.* It was Jalise, my assistant.

Salina was in her own world, I grabbed her by her face and gave her stern eyes getting her attention and physically demanding her to stop while trying to remain quiet. I gathered my clothes and quickly returned my button down on my back and my trousers back to where it belonged. As I got up from my seat, I gestured for her to stay hidden on the floor behind my desk. Before I could reach the door to open it, the phone started ringing. I ignored it and continued towards the door. When I unlocked and opened the door Jalise turned around and looked at me. She knew something was up, it showed. "My bad Jalise, I took a nap since I came to work early this morning and just didn't want to be bothered. What's up? What do you need?"

"Mr. Bates is here, *rememberrrr*, meeting this morning," confusion filled her body language as she turned her head to the left and left her eyes remaining on me. Caught up in the moment, Mr. Bates was left waiting for me to get it together. *Fuck!* Figuring out how to get Salina back to her desk without Jalise nosy ass noticing was the challenge. There really was no point because the chance that she had already seen her come in was great, but I didn't want to take any chances either. When I returned back to my office and shut the door, Salina was standing there butt ass naked, with nothing on but her pumps. This girl was crazy. "So, you didn't have enough?"

She looked at me seductively answering my question in every way but verbal. I put my hand up gesturing for her to stop as she started towards me. "Put your damn clothes on and get back to work man you heard that girl say my client was in." Disappointed, she walked back over to where her clothes were still trying to seduce me as she bent straight over legs still straight to pick up her clothes. I smirked a little. I knew Salina was a little extra but right now she was just doing the most. After fixing herself up she graciously walked out of my office as if trying to be seen. I couldn't do nothing but shake my head and keep along with my meeting. I returned, briefly straightened up then called for Mr. Bates. The meeting was brief, as soon as we completed it was almost time for me to pick Talyn up from school.

Talyn sped to the car when she saw me pull in. Excitement filled her spirit, she knew when it was just the two of us I allowed her to have her way. I tried my best to get her out of it but it was difficult, those big glossy hazel eyes would just stare at me pleading its case with the help of her hands clasped to add to how adorable she was. You just couldn't say no to that face. Taking the easy way out, we stopped to get pizza for dinner and a movie from the red box. Tamia didn't have that, so we took advantage of her absence and enjoyed an unhealthy meal for once. We didn't waste any time when we arrived home, Talyn rushed into the house dropped her back pack, placed the DVD in the player, retrieved ranch dressing from the refrigerator and took her seat at her table in front of the TV. My baby girl was growing up; she didn't need my assistance to do anything.

Upon completion, we attended to her homework and I immediately got her ready for bed. It wasn't the norm sleeping without Tamia next to me but I definitely enjoyed a break from having my arm numb and waste strapped with no room to breathe. The following morning Talyn was happy to dress herself. Tamia would normally have her clothes laid out the night before but since Talyn didn't have that luxury at her leisure she was pleased to be able to dress herself this morning. She picked out her favorite purple Tutu skirt that she loved wearing around the house since her mother rarely let her wear it out, purple tights, a rainbow shirt and her favorite twinkle toe shoes. Her attire was very colorful but I think it was decent. If that's how she chooses to express herself so be it. Prior to dropping her off to school we stop by McDonalds and grab some breakfast first.

     Although Tonya and Tamia were near the beaches, they preferred to lay out by the poolside underneath the gazebo. Tamia's new Tom Ford shades accented her attire adding to her model appearance. They were strutting around in their new bathing suits with confidence. Tonya had a really nice body but for some odd reason she was self-conscious. After a good amount of time of boosting her esteem and uplifting Tonya, Tamia was finally able to convince her to wear her two-piece swim suit without her overthrow that you would have sworn was a long Maxi dress. The weather was nice, the sun was shining bright and there were a lot of people out by the pool side this morning. Women in their thong bikinis, '*the nerve*' Tonya thought and the men were prancing around in their trunks and some even less. Everyone was looking good; you would have thought it was a swim suit model convention.

"How are you ladies doing?" This handsome bright skinned man stopped in his tracks to greet them as he openly admired Tonya's physique. Tamia was almost ashamed to respond as she admired his molded body through her Tom Fords. "We're fine thank you." Tamia replied as Tonya just smiled and looked back into her Nook as if to be reading. Tonya was still so frenzied by Rodney that she couldn't even assemble enough friendliness to speak to a man. She still felt obligated but little did she know Tamia was plotting to get her out of that and the perfect opportunity appeared without effort. "You ladies aren't from around here are you?" He stood before them to make brief conversation. Tamia sat up, diluting the awkwardness, "Is it really that obvious?" "I mean we do have a lot of tourist but as for the locals we don't have too many beautiful women like you two hanging around here," he said as he walked over to the closest pool chair and took a seat. "Thank you," Tamia looked at Tonya and laughed. "We're flattered."

Tamia was just being nice considering being easily flattered by flirtatious men was not her forte. "Is your friend always this quiet?" He looked towards Tonya indirectly asking her and once again she looked up, smiled and looked back into her nook. Whatever she was or was not reading must've been really good since she struggled to look up and join their conversation.

Tamia placed her hand on Tonya's thigh, "She's just being shy." Embarrassment consumed her in every way, shape and form Tonya looked at her as if she had just told her crush that she liked him. "What?" They laughed at her. "It's cool, so what are you ladies getting into tonight?" "I don't know what's usually popping on a Monday?" "A lot, the bars are always jumping around here. We have lounges if you like the chill vibe and one of my partnas hosts Man Crush Mondays at Club Tornado. Corny I know but it's usually jam packed. Y'all should come through." "So I'm guessing you're from here then?" "Yeah I just recently moved her a few years back on a promotion deal but after I was done with that I decided to just stay around." "Oh, okay I see, well we'll look into it. We're leaving tomorrow night so might as well make the best of tonight. You down Tonya?" Tamia wasn't really into the club scene but this trip didn't call for the norm. She was hoping Tonya would want to go but even if she wasn't, she was going to go and have a good time if it was left up to Tamia. "Take my number down; let me know what y'all trying to do." "Okay. Tonya put his number in your phone I left mine in the room." She knew exactly what Tamia was up to the way she looked at her as she grabbed her phone. Tamia didn't go anywhere without her phone. Tonya briefly gave Tamia the eye and smirked at her at the same time as she put his number in her phone. 'You bitch' Tonya thought as she kept a poker face. "What is your name?" "She talks!" He smiles hard showing off his pearly white teeth. "Nicholas, but call me Nick." "This is Tonya." Tamia interrupts. Tonya returns a smile unintentionally as they shake his hand, "Hope to see you ladies later and you have a beautiful smile, you should try it more often." He smiled at Tonya and walked away.

"I thought you were going to sit there looking like

you were sucking on prune juice the whole time. Dang, would it kill you to be cordial?" "Yes, actually it would." Tamia didn't expect that response. Tonya held it for a second until she finally cracked and they both fell into laughter. "He was too damn fine, I couldn't refrain myself."

"And I think he wants you."

"I doubt it he was all in your face the whole time, you better be careful Mrs. Suthers." "I don't need you to remind me, and of course he was talking to me the whole time that's because you were over there trying to act like you were reading. If I didn't know any better, you could've fooled me." Tamia rose from her chair and walked over to the bar to get them more margaritas. They stayed by the pool for the rest of the day until they were ready to go out.

Tamia asked Tonya to text Nick and let him know that they'd be going to Club Tornado tonight. Nick seemed excited once he heard the news and told them that he'd let the bouncer know so they don't have to wait in line. Her red dress was lying flat and ironed and ready for wear. All she had to do was shower, do her make up and get dressed since her hair was already done. Tamia was natural anyways so she decided to just go for a wash and go look. Tonya on the other hand had this really sexy two-piece outfit: a high waste fitted nude skirt and a denim skinny strap top with the back in the shape of a V. It was stylish, simple and original. She pulled her hair up into a high bun and wore a nude lip. The nude heels were paired well. She didn't need any extraordinary shoes considering the top made a statement alone. Tamia on the other hand went for her black red bottoms and a black and red ombre lip. They were ready for the night.

They cruised down the highway jamming the finest 90s tunes. Tamia loved her some 90s music. The ladies stood out from everyone in the crowd, you could tell they weren't from around there from their classy attire alone compared to the women waiting in line. Nicholas was standing at the front waiting for them. His chin met with his neck at the sight of them and his eyes widened when he laid his eyes upon Tonya. "You look beautiful," he appeared surprised. Tonya cleaned up very well considering the last time he saw her. "You look nice too Tamia." "Thank you," she said. "You don't look too bad yourself. He placed his arm around her upper back as he pointed towards the entrance and let them inside. The LED lights illuminated the place, it was spacious and the music was loud, a hip-hop techno vibe. People were dancing everywhere; you could barely walk through. Nick must've been someone important, when he walked through the crowd people greeted him and moved aside as he escorted the ladies inside his VIP. The ladies stepped into the VIP and took a seat in the booth then suddenly a loud unidentifiable noise at the time over tuned the music and lava appeared upon the walls. No wonder they called it Club Tornado. "This place is nice." Tamia spoke loudly into Tonya's ear. She nodded her head agreeing.

"What can I get you ladies?" Nick walked a waiter over to us and told them to order whatever they like. Tamia asked for a Hennessey and Coke while Tonya ordered a Patron Margarita. "Is that all," he reassured the ladies their order. Nick ordered a bottle of Hennessey and a bottle of Patron. The waiter attended to their orders.

"Okay!" Tamia said inquiring that Nick was trying to show off. Tonya looked at her uninterested. Nick introduced the ladies to his homeboys whom returned back from presumably the dance floor or the bar from their excitement. They were brief with greeting them and back to turning up. The waiter returned with their bottles as well as a bottle of coke and cups. Tamia didn't waste any time finishing her drink. She was determined to enjoy herself tonight but she was more determined to make sure Tonya had a good time.

"Please loosen up. You look good you should feel good. Take a shot with me." "I like the sound of that," Nick insisted. He poured everyone a shot and placed them on the table. "Let's Go!"

Tamia, Tonya, and Nicholas toasted to a

wonderful night and took their shot. Nicholas kept pouring them and Tamia continuously applied peer pressure and Tonya kept drinking. Before you knew it, Tonya and Tamia were both on the dance floor getting down. Nicholas joined them there and made his way over to dance with Tonya. She had finally lightened up and let go. She appeared to be enjoying herself the way she was grinding on him. Nicholas was being such a gentleman with her. Tonya was so drunk she wasn't even aware of her appearance nor did she seem to care, as her skirt continuously lifted he pulled it down for her. She became exhausted from dancing so she stumbled her way back to the VIP; Nick caught her mid-transit and escorted her back. She sat down and reached for the bottle of Hennessey, "I think you've had enough." Tamia quickly grabbed the bottle just before she turned it up.

"Give it to me," Tonya yelled over the music as she tried to grab it back. "I'm glad you're finally enjoying yourself but I think it's time we get you home though." Tamia sat the bottle down, reached for Nick's hand to shake and got up to leave. Nick escorted the ladies to the car and suggested that he followed them home to make sure they got there safe since they both had be drinking. "Thanks for the kind gesture," Tamia stated, "but I think we'll be fine." "I don't mind at all." He sat her inside of the car and walked towards his.

When the ladies arrived to their hotel, Tonya was slump so Nick picked her up and carried her all the way to their suit. He put her down at the door and walked her inside, as soon as the door opened Tonya ran straight for her bathroom. They followed her there. Leaned over into the toilet she was puking all of her lungs up. The sound of her puking disgusted Tamia, but she tried to maintain her composure. Her bun had fell by the end of the night and ended up inside of the toilet with her face. Nick grabbed her hair and pulled it together behind her head, "Go get her some water please." Tamia returned to the bathroom with a glass of water and was astonished yet comforted by the view. Nick was patting Tonya on the back while consoling her at the same time; he grabbed the glass of water from Tamia, lifted Tonya's head and poured the water into her mouth. She instantly turned her head back into the toilet and spit it back up. "Come on love you have to try to drink this you're dehydrated." She attempted to drink the water again and this time she succeeded. He turned around and looked at Tamia in relief.

"Thank you so much Nicholas, you didn't have to but this is really sweet of you." "It's cool, I feel like it's my fault anyways." Nick turned back to attend to Tonya. She laid her head on the toilet as if it was a pillow and Nick quickly grabbed her head and lifted it up. Tamia was shocked; she had never seen Tonya like this she just stood there with her face scrunched up. She felt slightly helpless as Nick was doing everything and that was her friend. "Hey Tamia, you're good I got her I promise I don't mind." "You sure," she asked again for reassurance. She wasn't comfortable leaving her friend with him but seeing as though he was a lot of help and she was a little tipsy herself she figured they were okay. Even if they weren't safe, Tamia had a 9-millimeter and a can of mace if he decided he wanted to try something. She went to her bedroom and decided she'd take a nap for a few hours then check on Tonya again. But before she did that, she took some ibuprofen back to the bathroom. They weren't there so she checked the room where she found Nick making her drink water again. She looked relieved yet deprived of rest. She took the ibuprofen then Tamia went back to her headquarters.

Reaching down to grab Nick's face while he took her shoes off, Tonya attempted to kiss him. Nick turned his head to the side, laughed it off and continued to her left foot. She didn't take that loosely as she leaned down and tried to kiss him again. He stood up after taking off both her shoes and grabbed a hold of her face. "What are you doing?" he asked her with a smirk on his face. "You are so, I'm just attracted, oh I'm-" She was speaking gibberish and Nick had a hard time translating her sentence so he just laughed. Now that she was sober enough to take care of herself, Nick started her a bath. The water was starting to get higher while Tonya took her time walking inside as she felt rejected so he helped her over to the bathtub, told her to get in and walked out and shut the door. As the sound of the door swung open Nick turned around instantly and was stunned at what he saw. Nick didn't want to give off the wrong impression, because his intentions weren't to have sex with her. Although he was genuinely interested in her he was still a man and the sight of her naked body slightly made him contemplate his initial intentions. He couldn't believe that she opened up so much after the vibe that she had given off told him that she had a wall up but he knew she was single after being hinted earlier by Tamia.

Water was leaking onto the floor as she stood there glistening before his eyes. Her hair was long, wavy and wet which added to the sexual attraction she had given off. Tonya didn't do herself much justice with her wardrobe considering she had curves and a nice sized D cup to balance it all out. He struggled to keep his eyes on her as she just stood there. No words, no movement, just her eyes analyzing his body language. She had a hard time reading him, but she never attempted to until now. Any man would have jumped at the mere sight of her and gave her what she asking for. But she was drunk and Nick didn't think it would be smart for him to do that. It wasn't before long that Tonya opened the door to expose herself after entering the bathroom. He wasn't sure if she took a short bath or if she stepped inside got wet and got back out. The second thought seemed more applicable taking into account the time frame. She started towards him slowly, swiftly, seductively. Not knowing whether to stop her in her tracks or let her do as she planned, he went with his first instinct and stood up. She grabbed his hands, rubbed it across her chest as the convulsions she instantly felt translated into slight hyperventilation he gently snatched his hands away from her. Her perky nipples hardened right away. The sexual intensity was increasing by the second and Nick didn't know whether to go left or right and leave before the heat intensified. He wanted badly to have sex with her but he didn't want that to subdue his judgment of her nor her judgment of him. Therefore, he snatched the throw off the bed and made an effort to wrap her with it, she denied. She started pulling his shirt off of him. He wiped his face and before she could get his shirt over his head he grabbed her by her wrist. She snatched her hand away from him and walked around to the other side of the bed ashamed. With her arms crossed she asked him why he was fighting it, didn't he want to have sex with her. There was obviously a misunderstanding as well as she just read him wrong just because he came home with them.

"Don't read too much into it, Tonya, I just wanted to make sure you got home safe." "Don't you want me," she asked bluntly, "because I want you." She licked her lips and crawled onto the bed. Her insecurities took over; he didn't budge a bit once she lied down on her back with her legs spread and arms out waiting for him to make his move so she quickly turned over and covered herself. "No, don't take that the wrong way. Baby you're beautiful I mean damn you're flawless. I'd be stupid to let you slip through my fingers but at the same time I'd be stupid to do this while you're drunk." "But I want to," Tonya wines while uncovering herself, "Can't you just fuck me already." It had been a while since Tonya and Rodney had last slept together and it was showing- she had longed to be touched. This type of behavior was expected out of Salina, but not Tonya. Tonya was more modest. The liquor was definitely doing all the talking.

"You want to do this?" Nick made sure it was consensual before he made another move. Tonya took that as a yes and crawled towards him. She helped him take his shirt off and proceeded to unbutton his pants. She lay back on to her back and in a swift movement he slid his dick inside of her as she cried out for more. His hands were tightly gripping her waist while he quickly pounded inside of her. Tonya could barely take it; her body was pulsing out of control. She grabbed a hold of his hands, let go then grabbed a hold of his arms, yanked at the bed sheets, grabbed the headboard. She didn't know whether to come or to go. The arch in her back raised as if she was possessed, her nipples lifted up to the ceiling and her head leans backwards digging into the pillow, she was enjoying every bit of it. She snatches the pillow from up under her and throws it over her face as if trying to filter the noise. "No, I want to hear you." He said as he took possession of the pillow and threw it on the floor. The sound of her moaning provoked him, he quickly turned her over onto her stomach and she got on all fours in the doggy style. He pushed her back down into the bed, he wanted her lying flat. He firmly gripped her waist pinning her down and slid back inside of her. She tried to grab his hands and stop him but he knew she didn't really want him to stop as she continued to sing 'yes, give it to me'. You could hear it in her voice as it was breaking; she struggled to remain quiet, trying not to wake Tamia in the other room. It had been a while since Tonya had an orgasm, and she could feel one coming on. He had no mercy for her, she begged and as much as he wanted to wait he figured if he was giving it to her he might as well give it to her right. He rotated inside of her making sure his head met with each and every inch of her vagina walls. Her legs began to shake under him and he knew she was about to cum. She tried to get up but he gently pushed her down again, he wasn't done yet he wanted to get his in. She turned her head around with her eyes closed as she puckered her lips gesturing for a kiss. He kissed her softly, quickly and returned to his position. He stroked her in one motion; digging deep inside of her and right away they came together in sync. It was all over him. He took his penis out and it wouldn't stop. Staring at her in adoration, he was prideful of his accomplishment. She was squirting all over him. She turned over, looked down at the puddle she had made embarrassed then looked back up at him confused as to why he was smiling.

"WOW!" She exclaimed flabbergasted.

"What?" he asked, "you act like you never squirted before." "I haven't." He wasn't surprised; he could tell that she had been deprived. He smiled at her then kissed her on her lips. Her tongue met with his as they began to massage the inside of one another's mouth. She grabbed his head and pulled him down on top of her. Obviously, that wasn't enough. He had introduced her to a feeling she never felt before and although initially awkward she realized what it represented and she wanted to experience it again. His fingers slowly trickled down her stomach as they made their way to her vagina. While he massaged her clitoris, she continued kissing him with such passion you wouldn't believe they had just met. Her mouth widened and she leaned her head back the moment he hit her spot. She moaned a different kind of moan; it was as if she was hitting a note. He started sucking on her neck then licking her chest, her breasts, his tongue made way all over her stomach before he arrived at his destination.

He grabbed both of her legs and placed them up in the air while he took his tongue and ran it from the bottom of her vagina all the way up her labia and then stopped at her clitoris. His fingers joined the party as he removed his t0ngue and began to massage her clitoris making sure to be gentle. She started to feel herself, touch herself; she placed her fingers in her mouth and licked them as if she was imagining herself to be licking something else. That turned him on even more so he resorted to fucking her again.

He gently penetrated her as he kissed her on the neck. He rotated in and out of her slowly. She grabbed a hold of his back tightly, gracefully caressing him as he continued stroking. Grabbing him by the ass she squeezed his cheeks and pressed them deep into her as she pressed back towards him. It hurt her so good she dug her fingernails deep into his back. She kissed him then held his bottom lip by her teeth. She pulled at his lip gently, pulled his head to the side then started sucking on his neck. His head rocked back and forth, she wasn't aware but that was his spot, his high. She pushed him up off of her and gestured for him to lie down. She climbed on top and briefly embraced his abs. She took possession of his dick in her hand, lifted her body up using her legs for support and slowly inserted him inside of her. His eyes locked with his as she cried a soft cry and looked away from him. Her body slowly rocked back and forth, up and down. He attempted to support her by grabbing her and bouncing her up and down on him but help she didn't want. She just wanted for him to lie back and enjoy her enjoying him.

Then suddenly there was a soft knock at the door, Tonya looked back then turned away she wasn't sure if she was hearing things or not. Tamia was damn near sleep walking but the alarm woke her to check on her friend after the drunken night she had recently experienced. Not thinking much about what she was doing, Tamia turned the knob, crept inside as she wiped her eyes clear she saw more than she was expecting and quickly walked back out of the room slightly slamming the door. Tonya turned towards the door again, quite sure that she heard something that time but she didn't see anything. Nick looked up with her confused as to why she kept looking back. "Don't worry about it," she said as she continued on her ride. Tamia returned back to her room feeling surprisingly at ease.

Meanwhile, in Jacksonville, Darnell was looking for a baby sitter so that he could go out to the pool hall with his boys. It had been a while since he had some guy time and considering today was Two-dollar Tuesday's at the Lounge downtown and his boys hit him up to go he figured, why not? It was so last minute and Talyn's normal babysitter Cam already had plans which she insisted on dropping but Darnell wouldn't allow her to. Coincidently at the last minute, right before he was going to change his mind about going he spoke with an acquaintance that didn't mind watching her. He had to think twice about it but he ended up going with it.

No harm, no foul.

Once he arrived to the Pool Hall, his boys had already made it through two pitchers and a few games. He went to the bar and ordered himself a shot of Hennessey to get caught up. They talked a good shit talk as they played and betted shots on their games. By 10 o'clock, Darnell was 6 shots in and ready to give up. "You done getting your ass whooped yet my brother," Kamal asked. "I think I've had enough, y'all boys ate yet?" Darnell didn't typically back down from a bet but he had to think twice since Tamia was out of town. They ordered two family sized Buffalo wings, fries and another pitcher of beer as they sat and caught up. "I'm surprised the wife let you come out on a week day seeing as how she with all that healthy living and stuff," Kamal joked and everyone else joined in agreeing.

"You snuck out the house Darnell?" Luke asked laughing although he was serious. "Y'all must be forgetting I'm a grown ass man, and Tamia's out of town I sent her on a retreat. I needed some space." "See, I knew it had to be something," Luke retorted. The waitress returned to their table with their food and pitcher. Miles didn't waste any time pouring himself another cup. "Can I get you fellas anything else?" The waitress asked as she filled everyone's cup prior to leaving. Miles just stared at her lustfully, but didn't say a word.

"You good Miles, you need some water over there. You look a little thirsty." Kamal asked Miles as he noticed the way he was watching the waitress. "Man shut up." Miles said as he downed his cup and poured another. The waitress stood there briefly, lost awaiting their reply for anything further. "You think you might want to slow down there?" Darnell asked Miles concerned. "We good baby thank you," Luke interrupted them and sent her on her way. "Aye, I'm grown too alright. Worry about your wife coming back whole after this lil retreat, don't worry about me." "See yeah I think you've had enough," Darnell grabbed the cup out of Miles hand mistakenly wasting it all over the table.

"Keep my wife out of your mouth too before you have to worry about me." Luke and Kamal looked at one another; they both realized Miles had fucked up saying that. They also knew that he was drunk and he didn't know what he was saying, but they all were drunk. Before Miles could say or do anything belligerent, Luke intervened and grabbed him to drag him out of the pool hall. He continued trying to yell back at Darnell and threaten him but they knew that wasn't going to go far. Darnell was pissed; he hugged Kamal and left out to his car. The music was already up loud and blasting Pimp C from when he was on his way to the pool hall so he didn't bother to turn it down.

When he arrived home he inserted his house key and unintentionally pushed the door open. Hoping that Talyn's babysitter had left the door open for him, he walked right inside without caution. It was quiet; you could hear a pen drop. Although it was past Talyn's bedtime he still presumed that they would be up playing or watching television. When he walked inside of her room, she was sound asleep bundled up under her covers. He kissed her softly then turned off her night lamp and left her room. Darnell wanted badly to get Talyn out of the habit of sleeping with a night lamp so every now and again he would turn it off in the middle of the night after she was already asleep and wouldn't notice. Sometimes Talyn would unconsciously wake in the middle of the night and turn it back on. It was as if her and the night lamp shared telepathy and she could feel when it was off. There were never surprised every morning to learn that her night light had ended up back on.

Darnell stopped before his bedroom door and realized the babysitter wasn't in the living room and although he didn't expect for her to be in Talyn's room either. He thought to himself, prayed to himself that she was not bold enough to be in his bedroom. He walked back to the living room hoping that he just overlooked her asleep on the couch, but he was right she wasn't in the living room either. The bedroom door had a crack in it so he peeked inside and immediately pushed the door after what he saw. Darnell could not believe his eyes. He had left one person there just to come home to find that someone totally different was in his home. "Are you fucking serious right now, tell me you're not serious?" Darnell asked moving his hands in front of his face surprised by her actions. He started to pace back and forth completely covering his face, hoping that he was just seeing things.

Salina was lying on their bed but ass naked with nothing but heels on. She didn't move a peek she just looked at him surprised by his response. After Jalise attempted to tell Tamia of what she suspected between Salina and Darnell and was instantly undermined, she had learned within a week or so that her theory was true. She no longer gave a damn to inform Tamia since she had been so disrespectful to her, and Salina was open enough to fill Jalise in on everything. So, that night when Darnell had text her about babysitting, she actually told Salina in casual conversation. Immediately Salina, started plotting to make her move while Tamia was still away. Plus, she was upset with Tamia and Darnell for not being invited to the retreat, so she saw it as the perfect opportunity to make a move. Salina had come over shortly after Darnel left and sent Jalise on her way. "Get the fuck out of my bed, I should've known you would go and do some stupid shit like this. Damn man, I didn't think you could be so fucked up."

"What Darnell? So, you're mad at me." Salina stayed right where she was, she only sat up with her legs propped open hoping to arouse him. Bold enough to sit on their bed, and even worse she didn't have on any clothes, Darnell was fuming with rage. He walked over to her and grabbed her by the wrist tightly and yanked her off their bed. "Darnell you're hurting me," she wined while trying to unattach herself from him, to no avail. He dragged her to the living room, quickly went back into his room and gathered her clothes off the floor then threw them at her. "Put your clothes on," he said while cutting the lights on. "And get the fuck out."

Salina threw her clothes on the couch beside her and stood up before him. She grabbed at his zipper and quickly unzipped his pants and placed her hand inside. "Man, what are you doing? My daughter is in there." "She's fine, she's sleeping." Salina stated as she continued on her quest trying to pull his penis outside of his pants.

"Stop!" he pulled her hand out of his pants.

Somehow, she managed to unbutton his pants also in the process. Salina wouldn't give up. Although, his mouth was saying no his delay in denying her services told her he wanted it. So, she kept on her mission. She cuffed his balls into her hand and slightly squeezed and pulled them towards her as she walked closer to him. "Man, what are you doing?" He asked her while grabbing her hand, attempting to pull it out of his pants. "C'mon you know you want to." "Look Salina, I'm not about to fuck you while my daughter is in the other room. What if you wake her?" Of all things Darnell was concerned with, he was worried about waking Talyn. It was as if he had forgotten he was more pressed to get her out of his home. She placed her finger on her lips and said, "I promise to be quiet. Actually, you don't even have to do anything just let me do all the work. Please, I'm sorry." She slid onto her knees and took his pants with her to the floor. Once his pants reached the floor she stood back onto her feet, yanked his boxers down, and pushed him onto the la-Z boy close by. Darnell was getting agitated but he couldn't resist her anymore. He knew she was about to give him fellatio and for some reason he couldn't pass up. As much as he wanted to kick her out of his house for disrespecting him and as well as his wife, he felt defeated. He lied back, allowing her to apologize the way she saw fit and made an attempt to talk shit at the same time.

"Don't ever do no shit like that again." Darnell said as she tightly gripped his dick in her hands.

She looked up at him, "I promise." She slowly dragged her tongue from his balls all the way up his shaft to the tip. "It won't happen again." She tickled the tip of his dick with her tongue while looking up at him at the same time. Darnell couldn't handle the pressure; he closed his eyes and leaned back into the chair. She slowly put all of him into her mouth being careful not to cause herself to gag. Salina was moving at a slow pace, stopping every time she made it to the top slurping the wetness back into her mouth. He placed his hands on the back of her head guiding her back onto his penis while finding a good speed. Salina removed her hands and allowed him to take control.

Minutes had passed and she barely gasped for air. "Damn," Darnell looked down at Salina making sure she was still alive and well. She noticed him look at her and nibbled at him answering his question. "Don't...." he said grabbing her head to make her stop. He felt himself about to cum and tried his best to pull her away from him. He knew he wouldn't though, it was just a tease considering how drunk he was, he was more so numb than anything else. She kept going for at least another 5 minutes while he continuously fought with her. She caught his arms and pinned them down alongside, looked up at him and let him cum all over her face. Letting go of his hands, she stood up then tried to sit on him but he wouldn't let her. "What's wrong?" she asked as she wiped her face and licked her mouth and fingers clean still trying to seduce him. Darnell stood up, took his pants completely off and walked into his bedroom. As he was trying to take a piss, Salina walked up and he slammed the door at the same time. Startled she was, so she opened the bathroom door to confront him but it was locked. She knocked on the door several times before he opened it to walk out.

"Didn't I tell you before that my daughter is in their sleeping? Chill out." Darnell took his shirt off then walked back to the living room with nothing but socks on, grabbed the remote and turned on the TV. It was like nothing ever happened. She felt as though he had completely shut her out. Salina was confused and didn't know what to do. She walked in front of him and he scooted over to the end of the couch so that he could see the TV but she followed and blocked his view again. He pointed the remote at the TV and attempted to change the channel but nothing happened. With her arms crossed she stuck her neck out at him pleading for him to acknowledge her. "Come on now, you see me trying to catch the recap, move!" With her vagina staring him down, she walked closer towards his face and her smell immediately disturbed him. Not in a bad way though. He scrunched up his face, "put your clothes on man don't nobody want to see all that." As if he wasn't naked himself.

She grew embarrassed yet she didn't allow that interfere. She tried to sit on his lap, but Darnell grew more and more frustrated before he snapped slightly frightening her. She hopped off the couch after being thrown to the side of him in a split second and preceded to putting her clothes on. Darnell began laughing.

"Ooohh, you are an asshole!"

"*I know*," Darnell responded, coldly.

After finding the scores that he sought on TV he turned it off and started for his bedroom. Thinking that she would join him in his bed, she followed in suit and was unfortunately in for a rude awakening. He stopped her as she tried to climb into his bed and asked her what she was doing. Darnell might've been a little drunk but he wasn't that stupid. Tamia was coming home in the morning and unless they both wanted to lose their lives, he had to get her out of there. So, he grabbed her by the shoulder and escorted her back towards the door. "Why are you being so cold?" she asked him as her eyes began to tear.

"Why are you being so stupid?"

"You are treating me like I'm just some side bitch that should know her place or something. Like this wasn't supposed to be us, our life, my daughter, our family." She cried out. Salina had been holding on to old feelings for Darnell and they were just starting to reveal itself in full. That did it, Darnell had enough. He wasn't trying to have that conversation again. "Are you crying? Man, you gotta go with all that. We'll talk later, you tripping for real shawty." He walked to the bathroom and grabbed her tissues. Apparently, he wasn't that cold. As he tried to help her wipe her face, she snatched the tissues from him and walked back into the living room and sat on the couch. "Look, I'm not trying to be mean or nothing but you have to leave and you gotta leave now..."

She sat cross legged with her arms crossed on the couch as if boycotting. After putting up a good fight for at least another 20 minutes she had given up. She was done being treated like trash and even worse she felt emotionally and physically abused. She started for the front door and before walking completely out; she turned around and said, "I'll get what's mine sooner or later." Darnell just laughs, tells her she's crazy and pushes the door behind her.

CHAPTER VI

Release

Demetri and Tamia briefly stopped by Darnell's firm since they were in the area on their way to meet with Alex Racoda at his workshop. She stopped to grab him a bite to eat before heading to his office. Jalise welcomed Tamia the usual way when she walked in the office, "How are you today Mrs. Suthers? I'll let Darnell know you're here." "Don't worry about it, its fine." Tamia told Jalise as she proceeded towards Darnell's office. "Mrs. Suthers? Wait." Jalise called to Tamia quickly before she reached Darnell's door. Tamia looked back at her confused. She then walked towards her once she noticed the concerned look on her face.

"Yes Jalise."

"Sorry if this isn't my place but if you don't mind, I want to talk to you woman to woman about something of concern." Jalise leaned in to Tamia and spoke softly, as if she didn't want to be heard. "Regarding," Tamia didn't know what the hell she was referring to but she definitely wanted to know considering she felt it may not be her place. If it was concerning her husband she already knew where that was going. Nowhere!

There was a small delay as she looked around before saying, "Your husband." "You're right; it's not your place." Tamia didn't like people in her family's business. They kept their relationship to themselves as much as possible especially when it concerned outsiders. She turned away and kept on towards his office. "It's not like that." Jalise tried to retract Tamia's attention but she kept to Darnell's office.

People need to learn to mind their business, Tamia thought to herself. Once she entered Darnell's office he was surprised, he wasn't expecting her and luckily she caught him before he headed out to grab something to eat. "Wassup," Darnell greeted her as he stood to walk around and grab the chair for her.

"No, baby its fine I'm not staying long, we're on our way to a meeting I just thought I'd stop by briefly since I was in the area anyways," she said as she sat the food down on the table, "How's work?" "Everything good around here, you know." Darnell says vaguely. "Well I'm going to head to this meeting," Tamia walks towards Darnell as he's sitting and kisses him before she heads out. *SMACK!* Her butt sounded off loudly as he smacked her on it as soon as she turned away from him. She quickly glances around, perks her booty, smirks and says, "I'll see you at home."

"Oh yeah," she stopped again forgetting something, "the weirdest thing happened when I walked in." "What's that baby?" Darnell asked interested. "Jalise tried to stop me from walking in talking about she wanted to speak to me woman to woman about something regarding us. She has a lot of nerve and you need to talk to her about that. You know how I feel about people in our business." "What?" he had a hard time deciphering because he was busy thinking about what it was she could've possibly been trying to tell Tamia. And unfortunately, he had nothing.

"Exactly my point," She said. "But anyways boo I'll see you later." "Aye, don't worry about her Tam." Darnell ensured his wife that she had nothing to worry about, which she already knew.

Wanting terribly to tell Tamia, she attempted to stop her again before she walked out of the door. "Mrs. Suthers?" Staring in the glass door she briefly contemplated turning around and seeing Jalise's face yearning desperately to talk to her, she went ahead and saw what she wanted. "I could be wrong-" "And you might be," Tamia says bluntly reassuring Jalise. "You and Salina are friends, right?" "Yes," she answers hesitantly disturbed by where this conversation could be headed. "Uum." Jalise had to think really hard about whether she wanted to even put this thought in Tamia's head but before she could finish speaking Tamia interrupted her train of thought. "Speak your mind honey, I'm listening now." She then put herself in Tamia's shoes and considering the fact that if she was her she'd want to know and said straight away, "I think Salina may be coming on to your husband. I could be wrong but-" She said quickly before being rudely interrupted. With a disgruntled and confused look on her face, Tamia took a step back, poked her ear out towards Jalise and said, "What?" "I know how this must sound but hear me out." Trying her very best not to come off rude, Tamia responds saying, "Actually you don't know how crazy you sound but I can tell you that Salina and I are good friends and her and Darnell are also so maybe there relationship just may be a little confusing to you. I mean they're like siblings." Tamia briefly explains their relationship and heads for the door. "Thank you for showing concern though, but I promise you we're fine." "Okay, I'm sorry." Jalise says aloud then whispers, "If you say so" while rolling her eyes.

Demetri was busy on the phone visually cup caking the way he was blushing when Tamia arrived back to the car. Just like that she forgot about her last encounter. That would've been some juicy information for Demetri to laugh about. "Who are you on the phone with?" she asks him loudly and he quickly gives her this 'what the fuck' look as if she wasn't interrupting him while he was on the phone. "Shhh," he says boorishly as he places his finger over his mouth gesturing her to be quiet. Disregarding his last gesture, she laughs and starts toward their destination. As soon as Demetri hangs up the phone, he turns the radio off and confronts Tamia regarding her actions. "Did you see me on the phone there or what?" Demetri asked her, pretending to be serious although he was joking. Tamia looked at him as if he couldn't be serious and turned the music back on. He clicked it off again. She turns it back on then he clicks it off again and this time he holds his hand over the knob. "Don't play with me," she laughed and attempted to move his hand off the knob. "Nope, not until you apologize. I'm on the phone trying to set up my date for later and you want to be childish." Tamia laughed at Demetri and told him to stop crying like a baby because he knew she was joking. "So anyways," Tamia ignored him,

"Who was it?"

"David," he blushes as he scrolls through his phone to find a picture. Once he found the picture, he placed it in her view, she quickly looks at the phone while trying to pay attention to the road at the same time then quickly takes a second look and snatches his phone. "Demetri," she sings while admiring the photo, disregarding the road. "Pay attention to the road," Demetri laughs and snatches the phone from her. After hesitating for a brief second, he then tells her, "I met him at the Pride Walk." Tamia was surprised. She did not recall seeing someone so handsome at the Pride Walk. Surprised she hadn't met him there considering he was also a clothing designer. After finding out his line of business Tamia was more so surprised that they weren't doing work for him yet. "Can I get a chance to feel him out first," Demetri stated. "I don't want to feel him out, I just want his money," Tamia jokingly said as they arrived at Alex Racoda's shop. Ignoring her, Demetri rang the doorbell excited to see this 'beautiful artistic Puerto Rican prince', which was the name that he gave him.

Alex Racoda was an author, musician, and songwriter. He had invited them over to his personal workshop where he likes to say, 'All the magic takes place'. Although it was a studio he did not live there. When they walked in, they were amazed by the layout and how amazingly organized it was set up. Before taking them to his office he decided to give them a quick tour of the space. It was beautiful. There were instruments everywhere, from a piano, guitar, even a drum set. Obviously, this guy was multitalented. The natural lighting accented the studio just right to add to inspiration within the atmosphere alone. There was a bench located next to the large windows with a Mac book lying on it. He told them that was where he sat and wrote his novels. The printer, typewriter and book shelf were placed adjacent to the bench close enough so that he could literally reach over and grab any resources he required. "This is nice," Demetri wandered off admiring the rest of the studio. Alex must've been very prideful of the area where he wrote his books. He waltzed on over there and remained much longer than everywhere else.

After showing off his original prints, he grabbed Demetri from analyzing this particular painting he evidently showed some interest in and escorted them to his office. They went over ideas for marketing his books and songwriting skills for approximately 20 minutes and Alex was already sold. "Donde has estado toda mi vida?"

Demetri and Tamia both look at one another before saying in sync, "Excuse me!"

He had almost forgotten that they weren't Spanish and quickly translated his words. "Where have you been all of my life Mami?" They laughed. Tamia was flattered. "I guess we have a deal then?" She sticks her hand out for him to shake clarifying her assumption. He shakes her hand as she gets up to leave so that she can keep her word in drafting up the contract as soon as possible. And that's exactly what she did when they returned to her office. She quickly finished up the contract she had recently drafted (taking into account she knew she'd sell Alex on marketing him) then closed up shop and headed to the school house to pick up Talyn then home to her husband.

Tamia pulled into the driveway surprised to see that Darnell wasn't home considering he told her he'd be home early today. Trying not to be so concerned because she knew he always kept his word she couldn't help but rang his line- no answer. In that moment she paused a second, Talyn looking at her mommy curiously. Out of nowhere, she quickly snapped out of it then got out the car and walked around to get her baby girl. Walking around the house observant trying to see if he had been home, it didn't look like it. Nothing appeared out of place, his drawers didn't look plundered through; everything appeared just as it was left. Carrying on with her daily duties, she attended to Talyn and ignored the fact that Darnell was not home yet nor did he answer his phone which went straight to voicemail. Plopping down on the couch in a daze, she immediately recalled Jalise's accusations. Knowing how Salina is she thought... *what if? Nahh she couldn't, she wouldn't. Would she?* As much as a woman may trust her husband and even her best friends, you can't put too much trust in a promiscuous woman. No matter how close of friends you may think you are.

Hearing the door knob twist, Talyn jumped up quickly and ran towards the door hugging her father once he walked in. He picked her up. "Hey baby. You missed daddy?" He said kissing her on the cheek. Before Talyn had a chance to answer he noticed that Tamia hadn't turned around to greet him per usual. Placing Talyn down, he put his arm around Tamia's neck and tried to kiss her. She snatched her neck out of his hold. Not realizing the firm grip he unintentionally placed on her she mistakenly elbowed him in the nose. "FUCK!" he yelled as Talyn jumped frightened. "I'm sorry baby," he quickly consoled her.

Tamia on the other hand she didn't even bother checking to see if she actually hurt him or not. Darnell was pissed. He quickly went to the bathroom to check his nose in the mirror- on the bright side he wasn't bleeding. Blood rushes to the sight; he becomes lightheaded then quickly walks over to the bench by the window and sits down. Slowly laying his head back, his eyes drifted closed as he pounds his head against the window. It was all happening at once, all because Tamia was upset with him. She finally walked into the room and noticed his discontent. Not even feeling bad, she walks toward the bed, sits and watches him intensely waiting for him to acknowledge her. Acknowledge his wrong. Acknowledge why all of this had even taken place in the first place. Only thing presently on his mind was pain. The migraine was slowly but surely intensifying. He saw her, but he didn't want to look her way. As far as he knew, she had no reason to act in that manner. Tamia wanted an explanation and she planned to wait until she received one. Whatever came over Tamia all on a day's notice, really changed her whole persona and he didn't like it. Ignoring her, he stands up and attempts to undress as his phone drops onto the floor. Catching Tamia's eyes, she picks his phone up throws it on the bed and starts yelling.

Darnell was aggravated, he was being treated ill-mannered for a reason he was not aware of and to make matters worse he had a migraine. All he wanted to do at that moment was lie down. She was not reading the signs nor was she no longer looking for an explanation she just continued speaking loudly. "Shut the fuck up!" he yelled, "PLEASE!" She looked at him surprised. Her heart began pounding atrociously and she became completely and utterly speechless. Staring at him in awe, she didn't know what to say. Before she had a chance to speak again he said, "Woman if you just be quiet and let me fucking speak, my phone is dead." He throws the phone at her and waits for an apology. And in that instant Tamia felt embarrassed. She had caused all of this commotion and drama for nothing. Instead of just apologizing and moving forward she had to challenge him and find another issue, "Cool, but why weren't you here? You said you were going to be home before me."

Darnell sighed, placed his hand over his forehead lied back and said, "Tam. C'mon now. I have a headache." "And I want an explanation." Tamia wouldn't have admitted it but after what Jalise told her she was bothered. She stood there with her arms crossed looking at him, disregarding the obvious frustration she was causing him.

"Look baby, there is no excuse for me being late I'm sorry," he told her to shut her up in a soft and gentle tone. Agitated he closed his eyes and turned away from her.

Talyn was busy in her room playing with her toys. It was getting later by the second and Tamia had yet to feed Talyn. "Mommy I'm hungry," she told her advising of her neglect unintentionally. Tamia was so annoyed she took Talyn to the kitchen and allowed her to just pick whatever she wanted to eat. Of course, she grabbed a lunchable and headed for her room. Tamia just smiled and let her be. Upon Talyn finishing her meal, Tamia decided to get her ready for bed and take it in early tonight.

The sun was shining bright and early - peeking through the blinds which were slightly opened. The light woke Tamia up. Yawning, she stretched her arms out wide and neglected to check the time even though it was obviously late in the morning. Still in a rubbish mood, she turned over and contemplated getting out of bed and going to work. In an effort to avoid moving, she reached her arms out as far as possible to grab her phone and check for any calls or text messages. Surprisingly, she only had one although not surprising at all that it was Demetri asking her if she was coming in to work today. Rolling her eyes, she threw her phone onto the floor whining. Thinking of how annoying her clients and employees are, she really wasn't in for it today after her night therefore she decided to stay in today. Tamia wasn't used to ending her night like that. After their petty argument, Darnell and Tamia hadn't said one word to each other since. Tamia being the stubborn person that she is, and Darnell feeling as though it wasn't up to him to apologize because he did nothing wrong, there was no telling who would give in first. They typically lived by not going to sleep upset with one another, but last night was different.

The sound of Rihanna's "Desperado," blasting through the speaker of Tamia's cell phone, almost scared her. It was Demetri again. He had sent her several texts and on top of all that he wouldn't stop calling between the office phone and his personal cell phone. Evidently, he was worried bearing in mind she neglected to tell him she wasn't coming in. Tired of hearing her phone ring countless times, at last she texted him back. Not content with a text, Demetri called again wanting an explanation. "Why are you calling me little boy," Tamia said sarcastically. He was interrupting her me time, which she rarely got. Demetri laughed it off and demanded a reason as to why she wasn't coming in like they had traded places. Jokingly, Tamia hang up the phone on him and sent him a text telling him to take care of everything while mama was a way and that she'd be back renewed and renovated tomorrow morning.

Taking advantage of her time off and to herself, Tamia took a long hot bubble bath. She deep cleaned with her favorite Fabuloso and Pine Sol. She rearranged Talyn's room and finally put up the décor she had stored away. She danced around in her panties and bra listening to her favorite jazz tunes, and gouging away her much loved butter pecan ice cream while watching Oxygen all at the same time. Smiling to herself, she realized she hadn't had this much fun alone since her teenage years. And she barely could account for it then since her parents were always blocking. She poured herself a tall glass of white wine, slouched on the couch with her feet kicked up and enjoyed her reruns of Bridal Wars. Before you know it, she was knocked out cold.

There was a sudden struggle at the door. It was loud, almost as if someone was trying to break in yet the knob was turning as if the key wasn't working. Tamia must've been sleeping lightly because it instantly woke her. She hopped up looking around panting, almost paranoid. Slowly creeping towards the window, she hesitantly peeked through the blinds. Before she could see anyone, the door burst open shocking Tamia. Left hand against her chest, her heart was pounding non-stop even though it was only Darnell. Trying to relax, her chest wouldn't follow suit. "The damn door must be broken," Darnell said slamming the door behind him. Tamia overlooked, ignored him and turned away. Before allowing her to get too far, he quickly grabbed her by the shoulder turning her around. With a firm grip, he held her by both of her arms and pulled her close to him. She remained petty, looking away from him. He kissed her. Like a baby, she forcibly turned her head to the right but it was too late. He kissed her again while unintentionally loosening his grasp. She unattached herself from him and walked back to the couch as if he never walked in.

"How long you going to keep that up?" He asked her looking wary while taking off his jacket. Paying no attention to him or his question she stuffed her mouth with a large spoonful of ice cream and dissolved it with a sip of wine. Unbuttoning his shirt, he paused asking, "Oh, it's like that?" That was the least of Tamia's concern; she completely disregarded his last two questions, "What are you doing home so early?" She asked him, eyes squinting suspiciously. "Because like you, I don't have a set schedule and I can take time off as well." He stated mockingly, smirking at her. Trying her best not to smile, she briefly cracked a laugh then reverted back to her poker face. "What's your excuse?" he asked as he pulled his pants down and threw them on the recliner close by. "Well I was enjoying myself until you so rudely interrupted me," she cocked her neck at him, "It's no coincidence why are you here, you're always working late?" Instead of just going with the flow, she had to satisfy her curiosity. "Since you must know Wife," snarling at her, "it's been slow lately, I figured I'd take a break let everyone leave early."

"Oh, everyone?" Tamia asked him rhetorically not really requesting an answer while making a suggestion.

He sat down fairly close to her and rudely she scooted over. Then he scooted over, closer to her. Trying to lighten the mood, Darnell continuously ignored her by tickling and kissing her everywhere. Tamia made it so hard for him. "C'mon baby?" voice so soft, remorseful. It didn't last. Before long he was all over her and she couldn't resist. He grabbed her and pulled her close, smothering her with his cologne. And he smelled so good, she was weak. They remained up under one another watching television until it was time to pick Talyn up. "It smells good in here," he noticed, waving his head from side to side taking pleasure in the aroma. "I know." Turning towards him, she kisses him, tightens her legs around his waist and lies on his chest until she falls asleep. Shaking her, she wakes groggy asking, "What." Peering at the TV screen she realizes the time then hops up to get dressed. "You coming with me?" she asks before turning the knob to walk out. Darnell places his pants back where they belong, puts just his top on then goes with her. "I'm driving your car," she tells him reaching for his keys. Darnell never let her drive his car, and it wasn't any particular reason. But she had a car of her own, so what was the point besides her trying to show off as if Lexus wasn't enough. In an effort to remain on good terms, he sighs then hands them to her.

Talyn was excited to see both of her parents in the car to pick her up. Running towards the car, Darnell hops out quickly before she could reach the street and meets her half way. Placing her into the car, he tightened her seat belt and shut the door. "How was school TT?" Tamia asked facing her before driving off. "School," she said sighing heavily as if she were stressed. "Uh uh," Tamia acknowledges her comment. Talyn caught her off guard with that reply. That girl was aging by the minute. She looked at Darnell to see if he had noticed what she said and of course he did. He looked at her, shook his head and said, "She's your daughter." They laughed and headed home.

Making up for lost time yesterday, Tamia got up early. She arrived at work before everyone, before the crack of dawn, before Darnell- although he's always the first one up and out, and before the birds were chirping. She parked her car and walked across the street to purchase her routine morning coffee: hot Grande White Mocha with whipped cream, caramel drizzle and a warm croissant. "Ahhh," she closes her eyes and relishes in the first sip of her coffee. Now she could begin her day in good spirits.

Fortunate for Tamia, Demetri had all of the paperwork she was supposed to work on yesterday laid out on her desk for her reviewing. As much as Demetri got on her nerve acting like her mother, or father one, she was more than thankful for him. She briefly surfed the internet while eating her croissant and drinking her coffee. To her surprise after googling Jarvis Rashad, she came across an article. A not so nice, rumor filled, bad mouthing article that happened to include her name. In regards to Jarvis, the article was a good look but not so much for her. It read:

Sources are saying that newfound bachelor Mr. Jarvis Rashad may no longer be on the market ladies. To whom he is taken, you ask. Rumor has it, his marketing agent happily or not so happily married Tamia Suthers, owner of Her Image may be having an affair with her client. Stay Tuned for an interview later next week with your very own Duval clothing designer, Jarvis Rashad.

Hot, fuming with rage, Tamia could not believe what she was reading. She read it over and over again until those words were tattooed in her memory. She was livid. Restarting her Mac, she counted to five, took a deep breath and turned her computer back in as if that made the article disappear. Going directly to the Duval Reppin' blog site, she noticed that it was the second article under Rumor Has It. As if things couldn't get any worse, it came as a shocker that this article had been up for the past 3 days and no one said anything to her. Without taking note of the time, Tamia didn't waste any time giving Shannon Taylor a call. It was early, she didn't expect her to answer anyway but she tried a second time then resorted to sending her a not so nice email. All she could think about was if she hadn't decided to come to work early odds are, she wouldn't have seen it.

Demetri was surprised to see Tamia in. "Someone must've had a good night last night huh?" He asked her suggesting she got laid. Wrong! Her morning went south drastically. She was zoned out. Wondering if her husband could have possibly saw it, or his employees, or any of her friends, she took a moment and thought back on everyone's actions. Whether anyone had been acting weird lately, or made any slick suggestive remarks. Jogging her memory, nothing appeared abnormal. Demetri looked at her, analyzing then walked a step closer placing his face in front of hers. It was like she didn't see him standing there. "Are you okay?" sliding her chair out from behind her desk, she quickly snaps out of it.

"Look at this shit," she turns the computer screen towards him and points. Demetri totally overlooked the big picture and started fantasizing over the picture of Jarvis. "Damn, they're labeling him as a bachelor now. He does look good." Demetri's eyes don't turn away from the picture.

"No," she said sucking her teeth, "read it." Head forward, mouth on the floor, eyes enlarged, Demetri was thunderstruck. "I never did like her. And who the fuck are their sources?" he lashed out. Demetri pulled his phone out and walked away. "Wait," Tamia yelled to him. But she was too late; he was already on the phone and ranting away. She just sat back and waited for him to return. Apparently, he had it all figured out and under control. He told her to wait a few hours and it would be removed. But that was the least of her worries, she knew once something was on the internet it could not be deleted. Her concern was with who had saw it by now. Jarvis was aware all along, and didn't say anything about it. *And an interview,* she thought *how could he?* Good thing they had a meeting scheduled. Unfortunately, the meeting involved business prospects but regardless she planned to squeeze in time to confront him.

Distracted, the rest of her day didn't go as planned. She remained bothered and inattentive. All she could think about was potential reasons Shannon would have for making assumptions as such; for disrespecting her as well as her marriage. Only thing made a bit of sense to her was the runway but even then, nothing was suspicious. Nor could anyone have known about afterwards. The thoughts were emerging in her head. Regret. Anger! Rage! She went back and forth calculating the possibility of someone, somehow spying on them after the fashion show. What if, no can't be. Demetri walked in and caught her sitting in despair. He looked in her line of sight as if she could've been looking at something in particular, then back at her. In a daze, faced forward, sitting straight and poised, her eyes were big and full, mouth slightly open, nothing could break her focus. Demetri even so much as walked in front of her desk, and waved his arms trying his best to retract her attention. He was unsuccessful. Something was heavy on her mind. "Are you okay?" He paused briefly, still no response, "I just know you are not letting this stress you out." He put his hand on his hip and demanded her attention.

He sits down in her client seat directly in front of her, clasps his hands together and stares her right in her eyes. "Stop being so weird," she exclaimed! "I was just thinking." "You were thinking alright," He replied. "You looked like you were contemplating suicide. Don't let that mess bother you." She sucked her teeth then put her focus back into her work. "You know you have that meeting with Jarvis and the twins' right? You better get it together."

Demetri kept Tamia on her toes even when she seemed a little off her game - he made sure he was there to get her right.

The twins were radio personalities from 92.8 The Flame. It was a new radio station based out of Central Florida; they pretty much covered the entire south east region. They were well known and had the looks of models. They went by Twin T and Twin D. Literally that was it. Their real names were Tenise and Denise. Twin T was the Dj for the station while Twin D was the main personality for the network. They used to play basketball for UCF; everyone thought they would've got picked up in the WNBA. But these girls were inseparable, they claim they both turned down scholarships because they always dreamed of being models and doing other things but rumor has it only one of them got picked up and she refused to go without the other one. Oh well, who knows. Now they have a big gig, which pays well and comes with lots of perks.

Can't beat that!

"I got this," reassuring him then gestured for him to leave her office. He proceeded towards the door then paused a second and gave her look that said she better.

"Hi ladies," Demetri greeted, surprised that the twins had shown up already. "I have you beautiful ladies for 10 o'clock right?" "Hey love," they said in sync then looked at one another and laughed. Guessing they did that a lot. "Yes, but we wanted to talk with the owner beforehand, that's not a problem is it?" Twin D asked in a slightly begging voice but he couldn't be sure. All he knew was that she couldn't have been being seductive considering he was obviously a part of the LGBT committee. "I'm sure that won't be a problem. Give me one second," grabbing the phone, he called to Tamia's office. "The twins are here, they said they want to converse with you prior to the meeting. Are you available?" Demetri sure knew how to switch it up when business called for it. Tamia lets out an abrasive sigh on the other end of the line, "Sure, send them in."

As Demetri shows the twins to the conference room, Tamia gathers her portfolio, goes out the side door to the conference room and meets them there. With big smiles, and open arms they welcome her into their arms gesturing for a group hug. Making sure to control her facial expressions and not allow her thoughts to come out of her mouth, she clashes her teeth then gives a fake smile as she hugs them. *I hope they're always this friendly,* she wondered.

"Have a seat, ladies," she pointed towards the other side of the table as she walked to her chair at the front. Inquiring her services, they rambled on and on for a good 15 minutes or so before

163

Jarvis showed up and interrupted what she could do for them to expand their brand. Tamia didn't mind at all; she was actually very interested in assisting them. Her problem was that they were complete blondes. They sounded spoiled, overly confident, and just lacked total common sense. She had a hard time talking to them because they barely shut up to listen better yet catch a breath before giving Tamia another example of how they could, Like Twin T said, "I know we can make you rich while you help make us rich". Tamia wanted terribly to end the conversation- or lack thereof, without coming off rude since they had good intentions. They just didn't know what to say, or how to say it. Luckily, Jarvis showed up before Tamia said something she might later regret.

Demetri had Lisa cover the front desk while he escorted Jarvis to the conference room with Sharaine. Tamia was surprised to see Jarvis walk in first as if he owned the place. Appearing excited to see the Twins, he greeted them both first with hugs then said 'Whats up' to Tamia with this look on his face. It was hard to read, but to anyone looking from the outside they would presume they had an insider. A secret. It was closer to a smirk, his eyes low, head slightly turned and if not mistaken he winked at her also. Feeling uncomfortable, Tamia greeted him like a new client, "How are you today Mr. Rashad?" Being awkward he just laughed then briefly made conversation with the twins as he sat down.

Evidently, they knew each other. This didn't come as a surprise at all; Jarvis was your typical ladies' man and he was well known in surrounding cities. He got comfortable like he was used to being there, he slouched down and placed both his arms on the arm rests.

"Now if we could get started with the business of this meeting," Tamia stood from her seat and got their attention towards her.

Upon conclusion of the meeting with the Twins', they agreed to do a photo shoot and attend a couple of their events wearing P.A.G. But that came with a price; they wanted material designed for them specifically. They didn't want to wear something shown in the fashion show during the photo shoot. Jarvis was fine with that though; he was apparently designing fashion for the winter. But that only meant that he had to expedite their clothes if he wanted the photo shoot done sooner than later, which they did. Once the ladies got up to leave, they told Tamia they'd be reaching out. She nodded to them and requested for Jarvis to stay after. He smiled, not knowing that she had other intentions besides what he assumed.

It was nothing for him to smile about.

Closing the door behind the twins, he sat down closest to Tamia and looked at her. That's it; he just looked at her, in her eyes with these seductive inquiring eyes, and didn't say a word. Twisting up her face, she disagreed and he immediately noticed. "What's going on?" he asked crossing his arms in front of him.

Pausing briefly, she clasped her hands, slouched towards Jarvis in her seat and said, "You tell me." Her voice implied that something was obviously wrong, though Jarvis took a while to get the point. But that was only because he didn't want to get the point. Tamia turned her head to the side, awaiting an explanation. "Man, I don't read minds, what's up?" Jarvis cringed. Tamia referred back to her computer, she left the article up on her screen. Upon laying eyes on the screen, she twists her face in disgust immediately, pointing her finger gesturing for him to move around and take a look. He looks quickly then turns to Tamia and asks, "What is this?"

"Look!" she said, this time with a sterner voice. Jarvis took heed of her tone; he looked at the screen closely. First thing she figured was that he knew what it was but he was trying his best to act clueless. Momentarily, she watched his face paying close attention to his expressions while giving him a minute to read the article.

"I've never seen this before," he sat back in his chair and looked away as if trying to hide something. "Why are you tripping if it's not true?" She replied with an attitude, "What do you mean if it's not true?" But before he had a chance to answer there was a knock at the door, then Demetri walked in. Tamia looked at him like he knew better than to just walk in. "Boss I'm leaving for the day if you don't mind," he told her, "I have some things to take care of and you don't have anything else planned today." Tamia shooed him and told him it was okay. Tamia returned her attention back towards Jarvis, "So you were planning to do an interview?" Jarvis told her she asked him to do an interview in regards to his future plans as well as their business relationship. Apparently, she spoke nothing of this article or rumors of them sleeping together. Observing how uncomfortable it obviously made her he made an attempt to put her at ease by clarifying, "Since when a journalist needed permission to write about someone?"

"That's not the point," she reminded him.
"The point is I'm married and I don't need anyone spreading rumors about an affair. Whatever you told them, clear it up and that's the last I want to hear about something like this or our business here is done!" Raising his eyebrows, he asked, "Like that?" "Yes," she paused and sat back in her seat, "Like that."

Analyzing her, trying to read through the tension, he was still content that Tamia felt something for him. He remained silent, didn't move a muscle, but kept his eyes locked on her.

She immediately grew uncomfortable and asked him if that was it as she wrapped up everything. As she walked towards the door, he slid his chair back quickly, stood up and blocked her pathway. Attempting to walk to the left and around him he blocked her path again. "Can you move please?" she asked taking another stab at walking around him. He blocked her path again, then again. They kept this up for a short time before she got the point and just gave up. "What?" she asked while looking him in the face appearing anguish. They locked eyes; his seducing, hers confused and weary. Butterflies fluttering around in her stomach, she grew ill. Ignoring the signs, she snatched away. "What are you doing?" Throwing his hands up in submission, he gave her room to walk away. But something weird happened. She didn't move a beat. That only reassured him of what he already believed. Grabbing her by the waist, he pulled her close and placed his lips on hers. Unaware that she had already given up and given in, he waited a split second before going in. But she kissed him back and that started the clock.

Walking forward, he guided her towards the desk. Holding his head, she fell back on the table as her legs unintentionally propped up and open. Once she was lying flat, he stood up and peaked underneath her skirt. A smile appeared on his face, embarrassing her she looked away. But he caught her smirk and that gave him the green light. He moved even closer, his dick pressing up against her pussy she flinched. It wasn't a defensive flinch though, more like that feeling you get that surprises you when something turns you on. That tingle that you can't fight, but you try your best to not show it although your body acts on its own accord and reacts without your permission. That gesture that identifies that you like what you're feeling, and inflames him to turn up the heat. So that's exactly what he does. His tongue gliding across her neck, she turns her head blocking him. It was wrong and she knew it, but at the moment it felt right and she couldn't fight the feeling. She felt possessed, like someone that she couldn't identify with took over her body to satisfy their long for. But he breaks through and she faintly squirms about. She starts taking her shirt off; he stops what he doing and watches her proceed. Licking his index finger, he rubs her nipple as soon as it became visible, then starts sucking it. Her left breast cuffed in his right hand, he massages it as he sucks the living daylight out of her right. She looks down at him, watching him, she licks her lips slowly. He catches her looking at him and continues gliding his tongue all over stomach, across her naval, then further down. Sliding her skirt further up, he takes her panties into his mouth then peels them off of her never unlocking sight of her. Once they reach her heel he takes control of them with his hands and take them all the way off and places them on the floor next to him. Examining her pussy lips, he bites his bottom lips then slowly let's go. Reaching for her waist he places his head directly in between her legs then forcefully pulls her closer. The smell of lust and lavender immediately clogs his nostrils. Inhaling, he closes his eyes, takes it all in and licks both lips imagining the taste. Making sure to be gentle he takes his fingers and slowly opens her labia and licks all the way from south to north elevating her every second of the way. He glides back down then strategically stops at her clitoris wiggling his tongue up and down, up and down. She grabs the edge of the table pulling up to watch him. Feeling her move about, he looks up noticing her watching him. Her eyes blinking more often than not, her tongue out of her mouth more often than in, her breath becomes short and she makes sure not to look away.

It felt amazing: her heartbeat hasty, tingles rapidly enwrapping her spine, her waist pulsing without consent, it was bitter sweet. Then suddenly his tongue makes entry where it didn't quite belong. She inhaled deeply and caught her breath, then let out this long soft sigh. He stops and asks if she likes. But she doesn't say a word she just remains quiet and looks away. Shame! Guilt! She was thinking of her husband through it and didn't want to make the mistake of calling Jarvis his name so she tried her best to remain silent.

This didn't last very long. She was moaning out for mercy as soon as Jarvis penetrated. "Damn," he says grinning as her vagina walls wrap around his dick like a glove. The tightness of her pussy caught him by surprise being that she is married. On the other hand, the wetness extracted even more desire than he was already prescribed from her sophistication alone. He begins by teasing her, deliberately giving her the tip and that's it. Moving gracefully, he rocked back and forth just a little. She rocked with him and as soon as she rocked too far all of him went deep inside of her and she let out this sound, like her breath was taken away. Stopping her from rocking he gripped her directly above her ass, his thumbs imprinted in her pelvis he did all the work. Stroking her slowly yet deeply, she continuously tried to assist him. Every time he clapped against her, she let out the same sound. If he hadn't known any better, he would have thought he was hurting her. But he knew better, he knew she liked it. Not once did she say stop, the moans, sighs, the groans all spoke for her. Her actions revealed what words couldn't. BANG! The sound of her slapping the edge of the table hard, with force, she gripped the ledge of the table almost digging her nails. The feeling was quite unbearable yet favorable. He smashed into her deeply, rotating around as soon as her walls met his tip and her vagina enwrapped his shaft.

He was extremely infatuated with her and it would only heighten from here. Everything he secretly presumed had finally revealed itself: she wanted him just as much as he wanted her, her sex was everything, her vagina like silk (soft and smooth), only thing left on his mind was making her his. Not in much of a rush, he was hopeful that day would also be revealed with time.

Stopping mid-stroke, he leaned over to make an attempt at kissing Tamia but she turned her head to the left forcing him to kiss her on the cheek. Confused about her actions, he tried to kiss her again and she turned her head to the other side. Detecting the discontent on her face, he became as unsettled as she appeared to be. Taking a moment to analyze the circumstances he leaned back, kept his eyes on her while her head remained turn. He eventually became uncomfortable, so he decided to slide out of her. Moving expeditiously, she sat up, slid her skirt down, gathered her top and bra into her hands, then hopped onto the floor to collect her panties and ran around the table and started getting dressed facing the wall as if she didn't want him to see her. Perplexed, Jarvis pulled his pants up and continued to stand there and watch her with squinted curious eyes. Making sure not to look his way she walked out of the conference room speedily into her office. Following behind her, Jarvis asked, "What's wrong?" She doesn't respond.

Remaining at her rear, once he enters the office, he sees her plummeting through her purse as if she was looking for something. "What are you looking for?" Tamia continues to ignore him and makes path to her desk and starts plunging through it also. Anxious, she jumps the instant she feels Jarvis grab her from behind pulling her closer to him as he moves close to her. He whispers in her ear, "Are you okay? What's wrong?" She doesn't say a word; she just sighs like she's irritated. Throwing her shoulders forward, she makes an attempt to unfasten herself. His arms are around her waist and his hands are clasping his elbows making for a firm grip. She turns her head to make eye contact but she can't seem to twist around far enough since his chin was locked into her neck and shoulder. The moment he feels her fidget he presses his lips gently behind her ear. She continues to fidget and he continues to kiss her on her neck aiming to seduce her again. He says softly while kissing her neck after every few words, "Why are you fighting me? I just want to please you... I know you want me... just as much as I want you... do us both a favor and just let it happen."

"Ahhh." She lets out a deep sigh, heart rate slowing while sinking into her stomach she says, "But I can't." "You already did." And the moment he says those three words, she exerts great power and manages to escape his hold. Turning slowly she faces him and grabs him by the neck with both hands and says to him, eyes piercing his soul, "I cannot do this with you. I'm married." As if she hadn't already broken her vow. Forgetting her location, she grabs her purse and stomps out of her office slamming the door behind her. Walking out of the office behind her, his eyes are drawn towards a sad Tamia. She's standing by the reception desk, hands grasping the edge, purse still in her right her head is down and her eyes sealed. This was the first guy Tamia had ever cheated on Darnell with and she was feeling it. She hadn't even made it out of the door yet and regret took over. Pretending to sympathize, Jarvis walks over to her, lifts her chin up then the moment she opens her eyes with that evil look she's so good at he throws his arms up in defeat.

"Go!" Not taking her serious, he looks at her standing in the same spot and this time she says more fearless, "GO!" He smirks. "Please just go," she says more delicate and this time a small tear drops onto the floor. Losing the smirk, he walks backwards, throws his arms out at his sides and walks out of the door.

CHAPTER VII
If It Isn't One Thing

Drifting into a deep sleep, I was back there, in that office.... with him. Trying my best to relive that moment the way it should have taken place I involuntarily pressed my lids securely shut although I wanted most to wake up from this nightmare. It went nothing like I expected: This time I saw myself stroll on over to him while he sat up on the table, feet dangling to the floor. With his index finger he gestures for me to come here, and I continued on my stroll slow paced while undressing layer by layer. Legs standing firm in my Jimmy Choos- the ones Darnell purchased for me as a 'just because' gift- of all shoes I could have been wearing. By this time, I was in my birthday suit. With eyes lusting for more, he grazes every inch of my frame ending at my eyes locking contact. I look down in a shy manner pressing my chin into my chest, which was so unlike me but then again that was only during contact with Darnell. He grabs a hold of my chin and lifts it up until I'm staring him directly in his face. Then he pinches it lightly, guides my face towards his meeting him halfway and makes love to my mouth with his tongue. Unable to let loose from his hypnosis, I give in. He stops after a few minutes then grabs my hand and leads me into the back door which led to my office, except when we went through the door it wasn't my office at all it was a bedroom. I look around the room at the set up and it all felt premeditated. I turned around and looked at him in admiration, flattered. Throwing him onto the bed of rose petals, I jump on top of him and ride him like we had nothing but time. After allowing me to show off my skills until I was worn-out, he quickly flips me over and makes love to me. It wasn't just sex, like a one-night stand, or a quick fuck, he made sure to be gentle and attend to every inch of my frame making sure I caught an orgasm. My legs began to shake uncontrollably, but he didn't stop or slow down he kept on. I felt myself about to cum, it was attacking me instantly, and it was making its way from my mind to my toes. Unaware of what might have been sparking on these thoughts and forcing me to dream such things, I pleaded to the 'Dream Lords' to wake me up.

Wake up! Wake up! I yelled in my head to myself. It didn't work. I felt myself becoming weaker, but in my head, I tried my best to remain strong. Refusing to accept the circumstances, I continued on my quest, trying everything I saw fit but I was under a hoax. A very strong hoax! While my body remained under his spell close to an explosion of ecstasy, my mind was somewhere else. My heart was beating fast in my chest and I was sweating out of control I could feel it falling down my temple. I couldn't decipher whether that was real or a part of my dream. Before I had a chance to experience a full-blown orgasm, I found myself awake. Sitting up in my bed, my hands gripping my comforter, turning my head back and forth looking at nothing; the moonlight was shining through brightly adding to the suspense. Surprised I hadn't woken Darnell, I took advantage of that and lied back down. Bringing the covers up to my shoulders, I turned away from him and just stared out the window at the moon debating whether I wanted to close my eyes and try to go back to sleep; risking a similar dream, risking thinking of that man-no, that boy- again.

I decided against that.

By the time I woke the following morning, Darnell was already gone. I didn't recall feeling him kiss me this morning before he left as usual. Only thing haunting my recollection was that dream. Thinking random thoughts, I tried to wash my memory of him. This didn't work; my head was all over the place. Taking note of the time, I hopped out of bed hurried to Talyn's room to wake her. "Ahhhhhh," she whined, twist and turned not wanting to get up. She was supposed to be up, have eaten breakfast by now and getting ready to leave. I couldn't be mad at her it was my fault. After enduring a brief struggle with getting Talyn up she finally complied. I quickly got her dressed, got dressed myself and left.

This morning I decided to sit at Starbucks and enjoy my morning coffee and croissant alone. I just wanted to sit a minute, think, relax and sip on my coffee in my peace without Demetri or anyone else interrupting knocking at my office door. After finishing up I walked across the street and inside my office. Demetri's demeanor did not match his tone. He greeted me, "Good morning Boss," while looking at me as if looking through me. I didn't waste any additional time looking into it, I said Good morning back and entered my office. Before making it through the door, I quickly turned back to him and said, "Cancel any meetings today." I didn't want to be bothered this morning, I just wanted to catch up on work and get my head together.

"What?" he asked surprised, but I know he heard what I said.

"I said," pausing, I smiled and repeated myself although I hate repeating myself, "Cancel any meetings I have today. Thank you." I turned away without waiting for a response, walked into my office and shut the door. Demetri was confused and wanted badly to confront me, I knew him all too well. Just like I presumed there was a knock at the door. Oh, I just knew it was eating him up. To my surprise he didn't walk in although my policy was to knock then enter. After brief contemplation I finally told him to come on in. He walked in and sat down in front of me. "Yes?" I asked as if I wasn't already aware of his inquiry. "Are you okay this morning? You know you have a meeting with Chanell Atale this morning right."

Chanell Atale wasn't anyone special- additional revenue. We could easily reschedule. Demetri was always worried when it was us that convinced a client to let us work for them and not falling through rather than them coming to us. He loved Chanell. She was a poet out of Kissimmee, Fl. Mostly spoken word and stand up. She had just recently moved here to Jacksonville and Demetri ran into her in the mall being a groupie. They became friends and he convinced us to market her. "Yes, I was aware I had a meeting. No, I was not aware it was with her but it doesn't matter reschedule."

"But you know we're--- Noticing the look on my face he sneered at me and asked, "What now?" "What do you mean what now?" I asked. "Are you still thinking about that article? Don't let that bother you" "You said you took care of it right? So no, I am not still thinking about that article." Before allowing him to speak again I quickly drafted an explanation although I needed no explanation just to shut him up and change the subject. He sat there staring at me as if I was keeping something from him. "Here's what I need you to do. If you don't mind can you check on your siblings in the back and see what they're up to. Make note of it. Then I need you to scrub the records and get back with me with a list of anyone we haven't checked in with in a while, an update of upcoming events, any prospective clients that have contacted us, you know what I'm getting at. I need that on my desk by the close of business."

His eyes widened, "The close of business?" He asked for reassurance. "Yes, the close of business." I repeated. "Thank you. Now if you need anything you know where to find me," I said dismissing him.

It tickled me a bit; he rolled his eyes at me before walking out. He was going to get it done so it didn't bother me, I just needed to keep him busy and out of my hairs. Plus, it wasn't bull; I would have had him do it eventually. Something had been on my mind a minute and lured me to Darnell's office. Playing it off, I asked if anyone wanted to send for food. Demetri allowed his attitude to force him to starve not considering that since I was leaving, he had to stay. Of course, the cool kids wanted food, and of all things they requested pizza. I had them call in the order. That gave me time to spare anyways; they said it'd be about 35 minutes.

Making my way across town, I arrived at Darnell's firm quicker than usual. I arrived just in time. When I walked in, instead of Jalise speaking her usual she made it awkward with this look she gave me. Then suddenly I realized what the look was for. While I was walking in Darnell's office, Salina was walking out. I smiled at her a fake smile and she smirked at me. She was still mad about the trip but she was mad at the wrong person. I hadn't talked to her since we got back. I had the right mind to wipe that fucking smirk right off her damn face. The nerve she had. I unintentionally looked back and noticed Jalise quickly look away as if it were none of her business. Which she was right; it wasn't any of her business. She knew exactly what she was doing though; instead of her trying to call Darnell and inform him his wife was in like she always did, she wanted me to see for myself after what she had told me. 'I told you so'.

"Hey baby," I closed the door behind me, walked around to where he was and sat on his lap. "Don't look so surprised." He quickly changed his facial expression to a genuine smile. "No boo I'm happy to see you, I just wasn't expecting you," he said kissing me on the lips. "Well are you ever?"
"Good point." He shifted around in his seat and moved me to a more comfortable position.

I proceeded to ask him what Salina wanted and also shared with him how upset she was about not going on the trip. He figured as much and went ahead to reassure me the reason I knew he didn't get me a trip for 3. Salina wasn't good company in the company of men. She was a bad influence and Darnell just didn't trust her. Could you blame him? We shared a laugh about her

181

being upset for not going. She'll get over it. On the other hand, I could tell that he was a little nervous and freaked out about my question in regards to what Salina wanted. He stated, "I mean she does work for me." Although he was right, I wasn't feeling his response. I didn't want to start an argument so I bit my lip. Not sure if I was seeing things, he appeared worried or paranoid. I stood up from his lap and walked around to the seat in front of him, I wanted to get a good look at him face to face. I wanted to read him, because that I did well.

He looked at me confused, "What?" There was a brief awkward silence after my mentioning of her being in here. Maybe I was just reading it all wrong because I believed a little of what Jalise said. But I had no proof. My accusation was solely based off knowing Salina's ways; I didn't have any direct proof like maybe she was always looking at him romantically, or she called him too much. I had nothing but Jalise's word. Saying something now would make me seem jealous, and I wasn't jealous. I had no reason to be, he was still MY husband.

"I miss you," I looked him directly in his eyes.

"What's wrong with you?" he asked, as if he could see through the bullshit. "Can I miss you?" I asked defensively although I had other intentions and he was right. Laughing he said, "Don't do that."

But I wasn't laughing and that was a dead giveaway but I couldn't help myself. I had to think fast and eventually came up with an idea that her time here was up- which it was. She had already been interning there for quite some time and he was paying her under the table but maybe it was time for her to get on someone's pay roll and not my husbands.

"I've been thinking and-" he interrupted me, "See I knew it was something. What's wrong?" "Nothing's wrong. I was just wondering... how long do people intern?" Automatically on the defense he asked me why I was asking him that as if it just couldn't be a random question. "What's on your mind?" He asked, "Don't beat around the bush." He sat back and got comfortable in his seat throwing his arms on the arms of his chair. This conversation prevailed just in time with what just occurred in reference to my thought, 'my point exactly'.

There was suddenly a knock at the door interrupting us. I looked back at the door then at him turning my head to the side, waiting. Before he had a chance to tell the person to come in; in comes Salina on her own accord. "Excuse us," I stood up and said. She rolled her eyes and walked out which really disturbed me. Darnell could see it coming so he quickly said, "Don't."

I looked at him and by the time I turned around

she disappeared. I almost had the right mind to have her join our conversation, but I decided against being messy and just let her be, for now. "That's my point right there, I think maybe it's time for her to move on. She's becoming dependent and I don't like it. She needs to learn some work ethic," I snapped. "Where did all this come from all of a sudden?" "Honestly baby I been felt like this. It's just that we haven't been on good terms lately and knowing the type of person she is I just don't feel comfortable with her working here any longer; for the sake of our friendship and our relationship."

"Our relationship," he repeated disregarding everything else I had said. "Yes, our relationship. She's disrespectful. Look what she just did for example," I pointed towards the door. "If you were feeling like this, why you didn't say anything? And baby if you guys are really friends you need to just talk to your girl." "I will, but I still think that it's time for her to go." Being stubborn, I crossed my arms. I had already made my decision. "Damn, it's that serious. Baby she's been a lot of help and honestly, I think you're just tripping. Paranoid, maybe?" He asks. Then to make matters worse he whispered, as if anyone could hear us from in here;

"*Are you on your period?*"

The nerve of him to say I'm paranoid and on my

period. Now I'm pissed. Fuming on the inside! "Really," I say, squinting my eyes at him. He laughs. "I'm not laughing Darnell. I don't know why you think I'm joking." He gets up, walks around to my side and sits on the table in front of me. I sit back in my chair and scoots back slightly. He looks at me and shakes his head. He's really taking me for a joke right now. Then he tries to kiss me.

"It's kind of cute, I never seen you act like this before. Tamia are you... Jealous?"

My eyes widen, my mouth does too. I'm at a loss for words. I can't believe he just ask me that and says that it's cute. I had enough; I grab my purse and make an attempt to get up from my seat. He doesn't allow me to go anywhere. He stands up in front of me blocking my way, so I sit back down and he smiles at me. "Baby if you want me to, I can talk to her. But that's fucked up; I can't just fire her for no reason." I speak louder than usual, "It's not for no reason. And it's not firing; she's technically an intern anyways." "How about this, you talk to her and think on it. If you still feel like I should I will. Okay?" Then he tries to kiss me again and I get this weird feeling that he's taking up for her and seducing me at the same time and I don't like the way it feels. It almost feels as if I'm not his wife and I'm asking him to choose between his mom and me. Maybe that's a little overboard but I have this idea that if your wife wants you to change something in your life because it makes her feel uncomfortable the husband should just do it. They say happy wife, happy life, right?

"I thought about this already Darnell, thoroughly and it's about that time," I say softly. I'm tired of yelling. His face changes from subtle to bold and he says, "Let's just talk about this later when I get home. I have work to do." I almost feel dismissed and this kind of reassures my theory of him taking up for her. I didn't say a word. I stood up and walked towards the door. Standing there staring at the door a minute I thought about what I might do if I opened the door and she were standing there. So, I got that idea out of my head quickly and Darnell yelled to me interrupting my traffic and says, "I love you!"

I turn away and it almost feels as if I'm saying goodbye but I'm not saying good bye, it's just my feelings are hurt. Just a little bit. Wanting to take it out on Salina, I walk out of his office and towards her office. But I forget to shut his door and since he's standing up now watching me walk out, he sees me and I feel him watching so I turn around. Noticing my look of sorrow and sadness he says, "Come here," and then meets me half way. He grabs my chin and kisses me on the lips, passionately and I feel butterflies fluttering away in my stomach. Trying my best not to look into his eyes, my eyes are looking downward so he lifts my head high and looks right into my hazel eyes. I almost feel shy, like back to my high school days. Then suddenly I feel self-conscious like someone may be watching us in the door way so I step forward pushing him inside of the office. I want to take him right now, but I know I can't and I know I shouldn't. I kiss him back and wrap my arms around his neck. The moment I feel him close to my chest, my nipples get this tingle and it almost sends a shock down my spine so I flinch a little. And he looks at me, smiling like he's up to something. I know what he's up to, because I had the same idea. But I was still mad at him. So, I tell him I have to go. Kiss him one last time and turns to walk out the door. He smacks me on the butt and cuffs a little in his hand stopping me mid-stride. He whispers in my ear, "I'll see you later." I walk out.

When I get to the car, I notice my phone vibrating in my purse. It must've been going off a while because I had several texts but I didn't notice. They were from Micah and Lisa telling me that they received calls from Dominoes telling them that their food was ready and if they didn't pick it up soon it'd be delivered to someone else unless they wanted them to deliver. They claim they almost told them to deliver but they didn't want me to get there and be upset because their order wouldn't be there. Looking at the time on the dashboard, I realized I had been in there for a good hour. It didn't even feel like 30 minutes better yet an hour. Time sure does fly. I pick up the food then head back to my office.

By the time Darnell gets home, Talyn and I are already settled in. I fixed him a plate, wrapped it in aluminum foil and left it on the stove. We already ate and from the look of it I could tell he would be coming home late so I decided not to wait for him to eat dinner. He walked in late as I presumed, spoke to me, kisses Talyn and suddenly a very disgusting thought cross my mind and I quickly dismiss it. The thought alone bothered me but I tried my best to maintain positive control of my actions in reference to my thoughts. It wouldn't have made any sense for me to flip out on a mere idea alone. That would've made me look crazy. I follow him into the room and help him undress as he unbuttons his jacket. He must've assumed I was trying to have sex the way he pulled away from me. Talyn was still in the living room and awake so I knew better than that. But the fact that he thought otherwise and dismissed it disturbed me a little. I took offense and left him to his business. He returns to the living room as I'm playing with Talyn. We're laughing and playing a game on my phone. He interrupts us and asks me what seemed to be a rhetorical question. And somehow, I got the idea that he just wanted to say something.

"Did you cook?" He asked, although there was food on the stove and the odor of the house answered that question alone. I didn't want to start an argument in front of Talyn so I answer him saying yes, that I put his food on the stove wrapped in aluminum foil and point at the stove. He turns away, retrieves his food and joins us in the living room. It seems he's upset from our conversation earlier so I end our play session early and send her off to get ready for bed. He picks up the remote and changes the channel as if I wasn't watching television. I sit next to him, not so close that I'm touching him but close enough that I can feel the tension radiating off of his skin. Leaning to the side to lift his feet up and place them on the couch he looks at me as if I was just supposed to move. I cock my head to the side and widen my eyes but I don't say a word, I just look at him until he got the point. Which he eventually did then proceeded to scoot further to the arm of the couch and rests his right arm on the arm rest. His entire demeanor from the moment he stepped foot inside the house disturbed me so before I have a chance to react off my emotions I get up from the couch and head to check on Talyn then to our bedroom.

Not sparing any time, I brushed my teeth, got right in the bed and shut my eyes to go to sleep. It wasn't before long that Darnell joined me there. I instantly turned over to face the wall, the opposite position from him. I could feel him turning over in bed, his hands grabbing me by waist and pulling me closer to him. The mixed signals left me confused and I couldn't help but continue to lie there stubborn, no movement at all. He was breathing deeply in my ear and I could feel it on my neck. It was slightly disturbing and hindered me from getting any rest. Before I had a chance to decipher whether to attempt to turn him over, smother him, or move further towards the edge of the bed I could feel it getting closer. Then his lips softly pressed against the back of my neck and that let me know he wasn't sleeping. He kissed me again and again moving closer to the front of my neck slowly proceeding to climb on top of me. Laying there inattentive, I didn't move a beat nor look at him. But that didn't stop him from constantly kissing and sucking my neck.

Maybe he didn't notice that although I was physically present, I wasn't mentally there at all. Darnell knew that was my spot and the fact that it hadn't turned me on like it typically would have I just knew I was out of it. He started sucking my nipples then out of nowhere he stopped. Although I was out of it anyway, I noticed so I opened my eyes and saw him looking at me confused. "What's wrong with you?" he asked. "The question is, what's your problem?" I reiterated. He snapped his head back in confusion as if unaware at what I was referring to. "What you mean?" "You're the one that walked right in the door with an attitude. What's with that?" He shook his head and ignored me. "Why are you shaking your head?" "I didn't have an attitude Tamia, I'm just tired." "Well if you're so tired then why are you still up?" His eyes widened then just like that he turned over and went to sleep.

We arrived to the photo shoot site bright and early. Surprisingly, the set-up crew were already there prepping. Demetri contacted Jarvis Rashad to remind him to bring the Twins jackets. He didn't answer. There were a few other models that were already there taking selfies and checking out the gear. We didn't have the twin's wardrobe because Jarvis had to expedite it and apparently, he had literally just finished. I hadn't seen it yet and I hope it was up to par. The Twins were so stuck up and boogie, I'd hate for there to be any issues with their wardrobe. I'd like to give Jarvis much more credit than that but last-minute things rarely work for anyone.

A loud horn blasted in the front of the park and before I could turn around, I could take a wild guess that it was either the Twins or Jarvis. Not because we were waiting for them to show up but precisely because no one else was obnoxious enough to blow the horn loud like that and hold it but them. Sure, enough I was right it was Jarvis. After our last encounter I was not looking forward to another with him. Being that I knew how to separate the two; that is business and personal I tried my best not to allow what could be perceived as a personal relationship interfere with our business relationship. I could take Jarvis far, if only he could get out of his feelings. If I have anything to do with it, which I do, there will be no other encounter like the last and if he even so much as hint at what "didn't take place" we can no longer work together. As much as I don't want that to happen, it's what best for my marriage and my career.

Especially after the bog post.

The prep team had to assist Jarvis inside the trailer with the other wardrobe items. We had to have portable dressing rooms and tents on site because the photo shoot was taking place at a basketball court. I was ecstatic to see what he had come up with for the jackets. Demetri actually assisted him in drafting the sketch and ideas for the look so I knew it was a sight worth seeing. We wanted them in exclusive wear and considering how popular they were in the Florida area and surrounding states we knew this would be big for Jarvis and his brand. The Twins wearing it alone gives P.A.G a lot of exposure. Demetri walked inside the trailer to inform me that the Twins would be here soon they just needed further directions because their GPS system was taking them the wrong way. I knew they were a little slow. Before they arrived, I wanted to take a look at the clothes they were supposed to be wearing. "Can I see the jackets?" I asked Demetri as he sat there on his phone as if there wasn't work to do. "Of course!" He stated as he pointed towards the closet. I looked at him in astonishment because he could've simply handed them to me considering he was closer to them than I was. But before I snapped, I took a second to think and remind myself to be professional. For some reason, he was really starting to get under my skin.

I pulled the jackets out of the bags and immediately I was amazed. You could see the twist of feminism in the jackets. All credit due to Demetri. I was sure they would love them. There was a pink one and a blue one, main color scheme being gray and white. They both were oversized army fatigue jackets covered in patches, diamonds, and studs. One jacket, the pink one had the letter T really big on the left side – I am sure for Tenise, while the other had the letter D in bold. On the back of them of course was the P.A.G logo. The jackets were different because they were high-low but instead of it being cut high in the front and low in the back, they were cut low on one side going long to the other side. The idea for the look we had in mind for the girls were tom boyish but feminine. So, either no under shirt at all or a sports bra, one with leggings the other in shorts, stilettos of course, studio headphones and maybe throw in a few shots with a basketball. But of course, we want to give them freedom of expression as well since they are wearing the look and they have their own brand to stay true to while marketing for P.A.G as well.

Regardless, it will work out well.

There was a soft knock at the door. T & D had finally arrived. We immediately started on their hair and make-up while Demetri shared with them the concept for the shoot. Thankfully they were with it, with no changes besides preferences of who wore what in terms of different styles. Which I would have assumed that either way. They were surprised that he had got the color exchange correct in terms of the pink jacket and the blue jacket in terms of their personality. Demetri was an image and branding fanatic so he could tell pretty much everything about a person from their style and personality pretty much at first meet. One of the main reasons for me hiring him as my assistant.

As the photo shoot persisted, to my surprise none other than the infamous Shannon Taylor had the nerve to show her face. If no one else knew what was going on around town, Shannon Taylor somehow was always aware. Before I had a chance to approach her, Demetri along with Sharaine had gotten to her. I couldn't believe my eyes, the audacity of this bitch to have the nerve and show up where she could presume, I would be after the blog she posted. Clearly, I would not be okay with that and at the first chance I get I will address her. But then again that could be exactly what she wants so that she can twist some words of mine. I walked over to where the photo shoot was taking place to overlook the girls at work and see how things were coming along.

"Turn towards the middle a little, facing the camera," the photographer said. As I looked at them, I realized he was talking to Jarvis. He had one of his arms on Denise's waist as if they were taking couple shots. It took me by surprise although I knew that Jarvis was just naturally flirtatious. They appeared to have chemistry the way she blushed and the way he looked at her. I wouldn't be surprised if he was trying to talk to or maybe even already was talking to one of them. Denise was obviously more feminine than Tenise... or at least that can be assumed from what meets the eye. Trying to not lose track of the reason I walked over there, I excused the photographer and asked if I could borrow Jarvis for bit.

Walking to the side of the trailer, Jarvis followed suit. "Why is Shannon here?" I asked him. "Did you tell her?" "Really?" he squinted his eyes at me. "You know –" I interrupted him mid-sentence, "You need to clarify some information she put in that article. I really don't want her continuing this nonsense." "I can't correct her. She's a journalist. It doesn't matter what I tell her, she gon' say what she wants."

Speak of the devil and he shall appear, she walked by at the perfect time to see us standing off from everyone else. Right place at the right moment for a journalist who had already made a story assuming something between us either way. This time I was not going to allow that to happen. Demetri and Sharaine were right along with her, looking around as if they were looking for someone. I assume they were looking for us. From their body language I could tell that things were about to either get resolved or get heated really quick. Demetri's facial expression told it all. He even gave Shannon the side look as he walked over to where we were standing. Barely watching where he was going, he almost walked right in to me. "Oh hey, we were just talking about you. What are you doing here?" I asked sarcastically speaking.

Demetri intervened before she had a chance to speak, "She was just dropping in to apologize," he bumped her with his shoulder. "For any confusion or issues she may have caused from the article." Shannon looked at Demetri quickly as if she didn't know what the hell he was talking about then back at me, and that's when I knew things were going to get heated rather than resolved. I had to think quickly, regarding whether I really wanted to handle this here while we had space and opportunity or be respectful and mindful of the business I had taking place. My money was first and I'll be damned if I allowed someone to come get in between that with their drama.

"Look Tamia, I only dropped in because I

overheard you guys were doing work with the Twins and Jarvis and thought I could drop in and get the scoop. It's all in exposure for you guys, I don't understand the issue."

That's when I almost went from 0 to 100 so I rolled my eyes and as I walked away I told Demetri to take care of it because I had to get back to work. Once I got back to the site where they were shooting the girls weren't there and neither was the photographer. Walking around a minute I still didn't see them so I figured the girls may be in the trailer. Luckily, they were I was scared they'd have left by now. "Where were you, we were looking for you." They said in sync and I thought I would have gotten used to it by now but it still annoyed me. They looked at one another, laughed as Tenise carried on.

We'd like to move on to our next look but you guys took so long we just improvised and finished the last set. I hope that's okay." I hadn't realized how long we were gone and as much as I didn't want them to view me as unprofessional, I'm sure they had anyways considering they apparently couldn't find us. "Where did the photographer go? I didn't see him nor any of his equipment out there." Denise answered, "I think he went to his car. He said he'd be right back so I don't know."

I called to Demetri to ask him if the situation was handled but he didn't answer the phone. After briefly checking on the ladies and making sure everything was okay with them, I walked outside to see what was going on with Demetri. Figure out why he wasn't answering his phone. And to my surprise, I see Shannon with a tape recorded up to Jarvis as he was talking. Something had told me that Jarvis had something to do with Shannon showing up today. Instead of him leaving the marketing in my hands I could tell after the fashion show that he was getting media happy and starting to let the exposure get to his head. If I find out he had anything to do with that article we were going to have some major issues. Pausing momentarily, just staring at them and into space at the same time I couldn't help but think that he did. Just watching his posture, gestures and facial expression he appeared to be soaking it all in. I couldn't take it no more I had to see what they were talking about.

"Excuse me," I stated as he was in the middle of talking. "What's going on?" As Jarvis started to speak, I couldn't help but tune him out and think to myself whether it was my place or not considering this was about him. Then I let that thought go really quickly after reminding myself that I was in charge of marketing him and I was the one that was the topic of that article after him. So, to answer my own question, yes it was my place. "What did you say," I asked since I didn't hear him after tuning them out? "What's going on with you," Jarvis asked? "What do you mean what's going on with me," I looked at him confused as if it wasn't obvious, "I told myself I would be professional and let it go since we are in the middle of business. I told myself I would wait it out and not handle it here considering how it could potentially escalate so I get back to work. Then I come back outside to check and see if work was continuing since I am paid for my time, I see you doing an interview. About what? Everyone acted like they weren't sure where she come from and how it is that she knew we were shooting out here and you're doing a fucking interview. I don't understand."

After rambling for so long, I didn't even stop to notice that Demetri, Sharaine and the photographer were standing within distance while the Twins were within view just watching me snap. I managed to turn around in a complete circle to see everyone just staring, watching in astonishment until I got back around to Jarvis awaiting a response. All he could respond and say was "Yo, you tripping."

Standing there with my arms crossed I look over to Shannon while she's just standing there with this smirk on her face. Glaring at her, I didn't say a word I just watched the way she moved. Before I could fully get up the energy to smack the shit out of her, I whisper 'I'm out' and walk off. I was halfway to my vehicle before Demetri managed to stop me and attempt to turn me away. Snatching my arm out of his hold I kept walking so he proceeded to walk with me. "What the hell was that?" he asks drastically as if I had really just showed my ass. Staying on path, I didn't respond I just kept walking. "Well since you can't talk, I guess you can listen." "Move!" I yelled as I opened my door to get in the car. Shockingly instead of him continuing to try to get through to me he backed away with his arms up and walked off.

The following morning the glare from the sun peeping through my window shade blinding me, woke me up from my slumber. Taking a wild guess before looking over to my clock, it appeared late in the day. Looking over I froze, it was damn near noon. 'How could I have slept that long,' I asked myself. Turning my phone over it immediately lit up and I saw several messages pop up along with missed calls and facetime alerts. Dreading dealing with the backfire from yesterday I turned my phone back over and got up to grab my laptop and check my email. Recalling how yesterday went down I was embarrassed yet lucky that I had my own business because I would have been fired. I am sure of that. Not surprised at all, once I opened my email the first message was from Demetri. I felt bad about the way I had treated him but he knew me better than anyone there so I knew he would understand and forgive me.

The text in the subject line wrote URGENT and I

was immediately concerned. Inhaling deeply, I paused and thought to myself what could be so urgent. I checked my phone and most of the messages, missed calls and pretty much all of the facetime calls were from Demetri. It had to be something important, Demetri would have eventually stopped calling. I'm surprised he hadn't showed up to my house considering how much he rang my line. I tried calling Demetri back but he didn't answer. Dreading opening up the email, I did it anyway and was surprised at what I read. I closed out the email then opened it again just to realize it wasn't a swindle. Anger wasn't even the word for what I felt. I felt deceived. Of all things I did not expect this. I had wrecked my brain considering what could be so urgent and this never crossed my mind. At this point I should have been speedily heading in to the office but instead I was stuck. I was in shock. I was in disbelief. I was.... Ashamed. Immediately I snapped out of it and instantly went into damage control mode. I have a daughter, a husband, a successful business and an abundance of clients that trust me with their presence. What sense would it make for a PR to not have control of their own presence. Everything was at stake for me.

With no time to waste I quickly threw on a pants suite and loafers and hurried to the office. To my surprise, the doors were locked, the lights were off and no one appeared to be in the office. 'What the fuck?' I thought to myself. 'I'm pretty sure my office is open. I'm pretty sure today was not a day off for anyone and I'm pretty sure the hours on this door says that the doors should be open and unlocked.' Remembering I owned the office, I grabbed the keys, unlocked my door and went inside. Clearly Demetri had been in but from the appearance of his desk you would have thought he was dragged out of here in the middle of working. His desk was cluttered and unorganized- which was so unlike him. This lead me to believe that everything else may be a mess as well. I toured each room and surprisingly everything else appeared normal. Even the cool kid's work space. Which was weird because typically they were the ones that were junky. Speaking of, where are they? I asked myself. This was so odd to me. The email. The vacancy. There had to be some kind of joke going on and I didn't get the memo. Pulling my phone out of my Chanel bag I gave Demetri a call. Still no answer. I try a few more times and still remained stuck with the voicemail. At this point I was worried. But if they were playing a joke on me someone was going to feel my wrath. After the email he sent, now this. What the hell is going on around here? I try calling Sharaine, Lisa, and Micah. No one answers the phone except Lisa and apparently, she wasn't scheduled to come in today because of prior arrangements but she stated she'd try to call everyone else and text me and let me know. For all I know she could be in on the joke.

I decided to take a road trip to Demetri's apartment all the way on the south side. After driving 30 minutes through lights trying to beat the highway traffic, she arrives to his door just to find that he wasn't there either. I was upset that he wasn't there but I was even more upset that I had wasted all this gas for no reason. *Once I get my hands on this fool, he's reimbursing me for having me worried driving up and down the street like a bat out of hell*. At this point I didn't know what else to think. It's only one of few options. He's dead, kidnapped, or in jail. Maybe that was a stretch but there were no other logical explanations. Knowing Demetri, more than likely he was in jail. But this still didn't account for Micah and Sharaine. Against everything I wanted to do, I drove back to the office. The traffic hadn't gotten any better and I was pissed. I just wanted to go home and wake up from this dream. Unfortunately for me, this was everything but a dream. More like a living nightmare. It had taken me damn near an hour to make it back to the office. By the time I got back, there was nowhere to park near the office and someone had the nerve to be parked in my assigned parking spot. I didn't have the time nor the energy to figure out who was in my parking spot or get them towed. Which more than likely, they would've been towed. There were more pressing matters that needed to be dealt with. I drove about a block and a half down the street to a public parking lot and walked down to the office. Luckily, I had on my loafers or else my heel would be in someone's ass because my feet would be hurting.

With laser focus and clearly not paying attention to my surroundings I literally was almost hit by a car while crossing the street. I was furious. This car sped up as if trying to hit me then had the nerve to hold down the horn. As if this day couldn't get any worse. Once I arrived to the office, to my surprise there was still no one there. It seems I was more so concerned about everyone's wellbeing rather than the email I had received that morning. The potential for something to actually be wrong at this point was pretty steep. I didn't know what to do. Mrs. Figure it outer, couldn't figure shit out and I honestly felt like I'd be better off going to sleep and waking up the next day and everything going back to normal. However, this was not an option. Something had to give. I decided to continue to my office and wait around just in case someone decides to show up.

Regrettably I decided to give Jarvis a call and see if by mere chance he had heard from Demetri. He hadn't. I quickly hung up before he spun my intentions as he loved to do. Although while I had him on the line, I should have inquired whether he had anything to do with the urgent email I had received. Surprisingly I was taking this very well. I am sure it was because I was in shock about the fact that something could really be wrong with Demetri. Sharaine and Micah were honestly the least of my worries. Knowing them two, they were probably together who knows?

After a few hours had gone by I decided to go home rather than wait around for no one to possibly show up. Luckily, today was Darnell's day to pick up Talyn so I planned to take the rest of my day and tend to some much-needed mental work and self-care. I pull out a book that I've been intending to read and finish for a while but I never got the chance to. Taraji P. Henson, "Around the Way Girl," has been on my must-read list for a while. This book would be just the motivation I need to take things to the next level for myself and for my business.

After about 30 minutes of reading Tamia was fast asleep. Startled, she woke to Talyn shaking her legs and tapping her nonstop until she woke up. Darnell stood behind her laughing. Tamia turned around as if unsure of who was standing behind her. She looked at Darnell as if uninterested then snapped her neck back around to tend to Talyn. Darnell, appalled and in disbelief walked into the bedroom and didn't say a word to Tamia. Clearly, they were still upset with one another from the night before. Tamia had so much on her mind that she didn't have nor plan to make time to read into it. Eventually he'd get some and get over it.

"How was school today baby?" "It was okay. But Ree Ree's mom is having a slumber party this weekend and wants me to go. I already told her you'd say yes. Can I go mommy? Pleeeaaseeee!" Talyn clasped her hands together as she begged for Tamia to approve her request.

"Well since you already told her you were going, I guess so, but I need to speak with Desiree's mother first." Talyn said okay then jet off to her room to start packing her bags. It was only Thursday but evidently Talyn was ecstatic about her weekend getaway. Honestly, I was too because after the past few weeks, I was starting to feel as though I was in need of another vacation.

Another night had gone by and Darnell and I were still sleeping on opposite sides of the bed. Darnell would usually be the one to give in first when we both were stubborn towards one another but this time he was obviously planning to stand his ground. And me, I had way more going on than some petty argument to resolve with my husband. 'He's not going anywhere', I thought.

Once I arrived to the office, I noticed the lights were still off and the doors locked. I walked inside to find that Demetri's desk looked just as it was left the night before. It had been over 24hrs since I last heard from Demetri. I walked to the back and to my surprise, Lisa, Sharaine and Micah were quietly working. "What the hell is going on around here?" I asked yelling while throwing my hands up curiously. "Boss calm down," Micah said as

Sharaine and Lisa continued to look down as if I wasn't even standing there. "Hi, Sharaine, Lisa... Nice to meet you too." I acknowledged them sarcastically. "Now is anyone going to tell me what's going on here at my office?" I look around the room stopping for a few seconds piercing each of their souls so they could feel my wrath. Sharaine and Lisa look at Micah as if he was the head honcho and it was his story to tell. "Okay so Micah I'm guessing by the look on their faces you have something you need to get off your chest?" "Look Boss. I didn't want you to find out before we figured out how to get him out-" Tamia immediately interrupted Micah as soon as she heard the words get him out. "Get who out?" I asked rhetorically though praying on the inside they were not about to say Demetri.

"So, Demetri-,"

I interrupted him again. I had heard enough. "Where is he?" I asked and, "why didn't he call me?" I scurried around the office looking for my keys not realizing they were right in my purse. Jail was no place for Demetri so I had to get him out immediately. Why he was in jail was the least of my worries at that moment. I arrived to the jail house in record time. As I approached the gate I instantaneously broke out into a cold sweat. Anxiety was catching up to me as flashbacks replayed in my head. I hadn't been to a jailhouse in over a decade and never had I imagined that I'd be going back inside one. Something about the sight of a tall gate, bob wires and security guards made me feel uneasy. Reminded me of the horror stories I'd heard from my dad. Made me think of slavery. Jail reminded me a lot of slavery. I took a second and practiced my favorite breathing exercise my therapist had taught me years ago. Inhale, 1... 2... 3... 4... 5... Hold it in 1... 2... 3... 4... 5... then exhale slowly counting down from 5. To this day, it has saved not only me from making bad decisions but also others from experiencing the heights of anger I could acquire.

After I gathered myself, I proceeded towards the gate where one security guard looked at me as if I had stolen his dog. I rolled my eyes and proceeded to my destination. Everyone in that hell hole was just assholes. I felt as if I was being treated like I committed a crime. Once Demetri saw me and he looked at me as if he had saw a ghost. "Nice to see you too!" I said to him in a sarcastic manner confused at why he was looking at me like that. "Oh, my bad Tam. Thank you for coming to get me it's just I thought David would be here." He clarified with sorrow. "Oh, that's who you used your phone call on?" I asked him disappointed. Demetri knew if he ever needed anything that he could call me.

"Tamia this shit is just getting way out of hand!" Demetri stated as he shook his head nonstop. I grabbed his hand and walked him towards the car. "I'm sure you're hungry, let's talk over food." "You want to talk right now?" He asked, shocked. "I thought you'd be ready to pull up on a bitch." At first I was confused. So, I asked him what he meant by that. He looked at me like he knew I had to be joking by asking him a rhetorical question. But it wasn't a rhetorical question for me. I was honestly in another world. He stopped mid-stride to the car, placed his hand on his hip, cocked his neck to one side and asked me what I had been smoking. I laughed. "Did you see it?" He asked me curiously. "See what?" "Oh, my god, Tamia you can't be serious right now?" He left me where I stood and walked to the car. "Why you think I was in the pin anyway!?"

Now I was really curious to know what he was talking about. We get in the car and start driving towards our destination. I leave the radio on mute so Demetri could catch me up to speed. I realized I had gotten only half the story from the email he had sent me that morning which read:

Boss! Get your ass to work right now. Apparently 'sources' have confirmed the alleged relationship between you and Jarvis. You need to get to the bottom of this before I do. If I have to call you one more time and you don't answer, I'm taking matters into my own hands.

He informed me that somehow there was a video

clip of me allowing Shannon and Jarvis to get the best of me at the photoshoot the other day. The video clip was reportedly vivid and clear. You could see me arguing with the two and hear every word I said with transcripts. Someone had really gone out their way to make this supposed scandal appear to be more than what it was. It pretty much made all of the accusations appear to be true. The worse part was that it had been apparently altered to say things that I didn't say. I was in awe. The side of me only few knew of was trying its hardest not to reveal itself. This situation had gotten way too out of hand and I was determined to get to the bottom of it.

CHAPTER VIII
Double Dealing

By the time Tamia and Demetri entered her office, she had just answered the phone and was a little too late. To her surprise, unexpected guests had just entered the premises and both parties could tell this visit was not a pleasant one. She switches off the music and grins as she speaks, "Hello. What a surprise! I wasn't expecting you all today, and especially not you." She gestures toward Demetri. Shannon was a part of the reason Demetri was locked up so she definitely wasn't expecting to see him. "They let you out already?" She asked sarcastically. It took everything in Demetri along with the strength of Tamia to keep him from jumping across that desk and digging in Shannon's ass. Although this visit was going to be anything but pleasant, they also didn't plan for them to end up back in jail.

"What is it?" Tamia asks with her arms crossed her chest. "What's the problem, because clearly there is some underlying beef that keeps you coming for me, so here lay it all out on the table." Shannon sits there staring at her computer completely overlooking them. "Um?" Tamia says as she slaps the table. Shannon looks at the table then looks up in astonishment.

Shannon tilts her head to the side as she looks Tamia dead in the face and says nonchalantly, "Look, Tamia I'm just doing my job." "Your job?" Demetri points. "So, your job is to taint my marriage? Your job is to spit all over my career? Your job is to be all up in my business," things were getting heated and Tamia had, had enough of hearing the careless words exit from Shannon's mouth.

"Actually, it is my job," she pauses, "I'm a journalist. It's exactly what I get paid for! To be all up in your business."

Luckily Shannon was able to get all of her words out before Tamia and Demetri took things left. By insinuating it was her job then proceeding with a brief pause, they assumed she was taking that in a totally different direction. Unfortunately, Shannon's job did entail exactly what Tamia was asking. Shannon literally fishes for juicy stories to tell in the area. It just so happens that Tamia had become connected with one of Duval Reppin' Blogs lead story- Jarvis Rashad. "Now if you could excuse me, I'd love to get back to doing my job." Shannon had almost saw a side of Tamia that would only take her career to new heights. Luckily, Demetri had just been released from jail so he was still freshly enduring post-traumatic stress from being locked up for almost 24 hours. Demetri grabbed a hold of Tamia and lead her towards the exit before things spiraled out of control as expected. Although, from Tamia's standpoint 'Shannon deserved everything coming to her'. Tamia knew this wasn't the most appropriate manner to handle it nor was Shannon the only one involved. As far as she was concerned, she'd take care of her some other time. As they were walking out of the office building, everyone was staring at them as if they were taking a walk of shame.

Which in a way, they were.

Tamia steps inside of the car and before starting the car she just sat there. Inhaling deeply, she grabs the steering wheel and digs her nails deeply into the steering cover. If it hadn't been plush, her nails would have surely cracked. As Demetri takes his arm to place on her back, the sharp fragrance perforated her nostrils suddenly capturing her attention and in response she throws her arm back making contact with Demetri's. He bumps her, then grabs her by the arm, but she doesn't move. She just sits there, with her head down on the steering wheel. Though still upset himself, he attempts to console her. But at this point there was clearly nothing he could say to get her attention. After a matter of 5 minutes, she snaps out of it on her own cognizance. Aware of the dimming sky, she looks up then over at Demetri, starts the car and says, "Come on, let's go. I know what I'm going to do!" "And what's that?" Demetri asked intriguingly. Tamia shakes her head and repeats herself, "I know exactly what I'm going to do."

By the time Demetri and Tamia made it back to the office, it was almost closing time. Everyone was still in the back. They both joined them in the back as they all greeted Demetri as if they hadn't seen him for years. Tamia was over with the day so she instructs everyone to go home as she gestures for them to put their things away. Nobody moved. They all just stood their stiff, looking around at one another. Considering their awareness of what had taken place they immediately bombarded them with questions about what had taken place. Tamia felt no need to fill them in so she simply walked out they do then they all looked at Demetri.

"I don't have time." Demetri says as they let out a loud sigh in unison.

Demetri joins Tamia in her office to check on her. All you could here was the sound of papers shuffling and drawers opening and closing. Tamia was usually not one to stress heavily over things that were out of her control. However, in this case she felt the complete opposite. She felt that something that had begun completely in her control had gotten out of her control. The thought of this put Tamia in distress. For a while now, she wasn't her usual cheerful self. She was a lot more stressed, uneasy and unorganized. In part because of her problems at home but mostly because of the current circumstances with Jarvis and everyone else. She knew that the only way to take back control of a story was to share your own story. So that's exactly what Tamia planned to do.

"Tam, you good girl?" Demetri asked as he noticed her rummaging her office like a burglar. Tamia had run lapse around the office in a short period of time as he stood at the door just watching her. "What are you doing?" He asked her again as he walked closer to her slowly. Tamia let him know briefly of her plan and against his usual judgment, Demetri was against it. In his opinion, at this point her saying anything whether agreeing or disagreeing would only make her look guilty and as if she were trying to cover it up and claim innocence. In part, she agreed because it was common that people would still discredit the person being blamed of something after it was already out there. He felt she would be better off ignoring the whole thing and killing her with kindness. It seemed that Shannon was reaching for exactly that and although Tamia was ready to give it to her, Demetri was able to talk her out of it.

"Look, just go home. Enjoy your family and we will deal with the rest of this bullshit tomorrow." Demetri was just ready to get home, enjoy a glass of wine, some good lovin' and relax. After one day too long in jail, Demetri was feeling as though he had some catching up to do. Instead of waiting for her to leave, he kisses Tamia on the cheek and continues on with his day urging for Tamia to just go home and as he would say, 'unwind'.

The skies were dimming by the second and clouds were beginning to flood the sky. Demetri hurried to his car in the back-parking lot where Micah had told him it was parked. Micah had held on to Demetri's car while he was in lock up. Despite the circumstances, Demetri managed to crack a smile at the sound of his phone ringing. It was David's ringtone. They were still seeing each other. He had grown impatient with David's attempt at small talk and advanced with more of a statement than a question that he would be on his way. As he hung up the phone and proceeded to drive off, he pressed the power button to turn the power on. Before he had a chance to turn off the radio and connect his Bluetooth he noticed two distinct voices. They sounded very familiar but he couldn't quite pinpoint who they belonged to. Until, they had reintroduced themselves. "It's your girl, Twin T....." one voice followed behind the other stating, "and none other than, Twin D." Demetri was surprised to be hearing the twins on the radio because he was used to missing it because he'd still be working. Fortunately, he caught them on air at the perfect time because coincidently Tamia was the topic of conversation. The Twins lead with this viral video of CEO or Her Image confronting Shannon of Duval Reppin'

Blog, and Jarvis Rashad of P.A.G apparel for apparently sleeping together. "But the real tea is…. that Jarvis and Tamia are actually having an affair. I mean I saw the video and not only that we were there." "Mmhmm," the second voice agrees. "From what we could see, it was a lot more to them two than just business acquaintances." The ladies continued on with their conversation beefing up the allegations.

Demetri was in shock. He couldn't even grasp the entirety of what they were saying to respond anything further than his mouth open and head cocked forward. Grabbing his phone, he gave Tamia a call. "Girl, what are you doing? Turn on the radio now." "The radio?" "Yes. bitch the radio, you won't believe what I am hearing. Turn it on now." Demetri pressed disregarding the fact the fact that he called her a bitch and she absolutely despised being called out her name.

"Now Demetri, this better be important you up here calling me all kinds of bitches and stuff." She exaggerated. Tamia was half way home as she turned her radio on. "What am I looking for?" She asked as she searched the stations looking for something that even remotely sounded like something she needed to listen for. "92.8, 92.8," he repeated twice rushing Tamia. By the time Tamia turned to the channel, the Twins had already moved pass commercial break and played the next song.

"Biiiiiiiitccchhhhh." Demetri held the word for so long you would have thought he was stuck talking that way. "Oh, hell nawl, let me call you right back." He didn't waste any time hanging up the phone to give the Twins a call. The phone rung several times then went to voicemail. Demetri tried again and the phone went to voicemail again. Tamia repeatedly beeped in as Demetri was trying to call out.

He finally answers the phone for Tamia and fills her in on what all the commotion was about. Tamia was speechless. At a loss for words. Not even realizing it, she had stopped her car smack dab in the middle of the street. Awaken by the sound of a screeching car, Tamia quickly got back to her senses and drove to the nearest street parking. Before Tamia could even gather any words to say she hung up the phone and proceeded to call the Twins as well. But this time, their phones rung only twice then went straight to voicemail. Tamia tried calling them a few more times until she was convinced, they were transferring her call. Before long she ended up back on the phone with Demetri. "Is today fuck with Tamia day? It must be, because I'm about sick of this shit." And at that moment, she snapped. She starts her car back up and crosses over University Blvd heading back towards her office where Demetri hadn't even had a chance to pull out from.

They met one another outside the car neglecting the fact that it had begun drizzling. On one hand, Tamia was ready to drive to Orlando and on the other hand she was just ready to give up on life. It seemed everything had come down on her all at once, including the rain. The perfect real life depiction of, 'when it rains it pours'. And in this case, not only was she getting her fair share of trials and tribulations the rain had also, poured down on her. They quickly ran towards the office. Struggling to unzip her clutch to take out her keys, she dropped everything out of her purse-including her keys. At this point, Tamia was truly over it. She stood up, leaned her head back and threw her arms behind her and surrendered. Tamia is wearing her usual suit, but this time a light-colored suit with her everyday red bottoms. She's natural, so her curls quickly drop then suddenly smacks her right in the face as she brings her head back forward speedily almost giving herself whiplash. Demetri felt helpless as he hurriedly moved towards the ground and grabbed the keys to get Tamia inside. With no care in the world, Tamia walks inside leaving all of her belongings on the ground outside the door. If Demetri hadn't been there her belongings probably would have stayed right, there. Slamming the door shut within milliseconds of walking inside her office, she couldn't even tell if Demetri was behind her or not. He wasn't. She plopped down on the accent chair in her wet suit with her leg thrown on one arm and her hair spread all over the other. In between the two accent chairs was an end table where she kept a stack of magazines, few bottles of water and tissue paper.

Trying her best not to move any part of her body besides her arm, she attempts to grab a tissue from the table. Instead, she knocks everything off of it. Her eyes unexpectedly started to glisten as her hands became clammy. Tamia was a blink shy of shedding a tear. All she could think about was her husband suggesting she had nothing to do with Jarvis. *'If only I had just left him where he was, I wouldn't even be in this position. This is what I get always trying to look out for my people,'* she thought to herself discounting the part she played in everything.

A tap at the door abruptly interrupted Tamia in deep thought. It was Demetri creeping in. He doesn't wait for her to acknowledge him as he goes into detail about how they will be dealing with this matter. He speaks fast, forgetting to catch his breath, paces back and forth towards Tamia then back towards the door. They both appear to be under distress. As his words begin to pivot to Tamia's family, this sparks a light in her. He waits a second as he notices she sits up as if she had just got an idea. "So..." he says awaiting her comeback. "What are you going to do?" Tamia hadn't yet considered the idea that she would have to tell Darnell about this, if he hadn't already found out. She instantly felt an ounce of remorse as she pictured a whole scenario in her head of Darnell finding out and threatening to leave her. She went back and forth between whether she should tell him or not because the fact that he would leave her if he knew was unbearable. The idea alone gave her anxiety. Confliction, denial, remorse, confliction, denial, remorse. She revisited these emotions back and forth within a matter of a minute as she considered the many different scenarios of how this could play out. Enthralled, Demetri watched her experience a minor panic attack. Her anxiety swept in like a thief in the night and sent Tamia into a whirlwind as she repeatedly asked 'what am I going to do?' allowed while holding her head. Demetri had never seen Tamia like this, he almost didn't know what to do besides console her with his touch. That was the last thing Tamia wanted- to be touched.

He walked over to the small table next to the chair and grabbed a bottle of water. Cracking it open slightly, he places it in front of Tamia's face gesturing for her to drink it. She refuses. This time he takes the top off and almost shoves the bottle against her lips, he gestures a second time for her to drink the water. Grabbing the bottle out of his hand quickly, she spills some of the water on herself. "Sit down Tamia, you're a mess. I know things are really crazy right now but I am not about to let you drive yourself crazy." Demetri implies. Even after spilling some of the water, Tamia doesn't move one bit. It was like she was in a trance.

This happened often. When Tamia is in an unpleasant state of mind, she mentally shuts the world out from around her. It hadn't happened for a while. The last time she had an episode was years prior. Things had been going so great for Tamia. Demetri yells at her this time as he places his feet down on the floor sternly, "Sit down". This time, ashamed, embarrassed, and aware, Tamia throws her hand over her face and sits down in the chair. She started repeating she was sorry. All the guilt of everything she had contributed that lead up to this point had come back to her. She was prepared to confess all of her wrongdoings. Demetri grabs her by the shoulder as he sits down on the arm of the chair next to her. He caresses her on the shoulder as he assures her that everything would be resolves. Her phone rings and Demetri quickly runs over to the desk to see who it is. "Fuck," he says aloud, "he sure has good timing."

It was Jarvis. Instead of throwing the phone like Tamia starts to do, she answers it with a very calm voice. "What?" "Damn, it's like that?" Jarvis responded as if surprised to hear she was not happy to hear from him. "You always talking about its like that. Yes! It's like that. Now what do you want, because after this phone call. I'm done with you and this business arrangement is over." Demetri looked at Tamia astonished. He didn't expect for it to go there. Jarvis called to inform Tamia that he was aware of where the video came from and that he was taking care of it as they spoke. Apparently, Jarvis ex-girlfriend Ja'lyssa had went to Shannon Taylor with allegations of Tamia and Jarvis sleeping together. She was upset that he had thrown her out of the Pride Walk. Instead of leaving she had actually stuck around and saw the two of them kiss backstage after the show. So, she invited Shannon to the photoshoot that she had learned about from the Twins and decided to stand clear to get video of any sketchy interaction that tied together her theory of the two of them sleeping together. Tamia was heated. She just listened and rolled her eyes as he spoke.

The conversation ended with an awkward pause then Tamia hanging up the phone. She stood up and walked over to her desk where the papers she had previously stacked was. Before she had a chance to gather the stack of papers in her hand, her body jolted forward as puke sporadically exited her mouth all over the desk. Demetri quickly covered his mouth and stood there in complete and utterly shock. As if this day couldn't get any more messed up, to add the icing to it all Tamia had just thrown up an empty stomach everywhere leaving the office smelling sour. It was at that moment Demetri knew it was his cue to get Tamia home safely.

CHAPTER IX
With A Grain Of Salt

Tamia was in no mood to attend the opening of this new restaurant with the girls after her recent incident. Tanya had learned about the opening of this new restaurant and booked them a reservation to one of their grand opening events. Tamia hated to be one to flake and it had been a while since she had linked up with the girls. Nonetheless, she whipped herself into shape and went anyway. Arriving early, she requested a table for 3 in the nook of the dining area where she could get a good view of the entrance as her friends arrived. She looked around the room soaking up the atmosphere. The ambience seemed to help her remain calm. Ever since her last episode she was concerned that she may undergo another unexpectedly. In the past when she would have these anxiety attacks, they would slither in unannounced. It was too soon to tell. Before she left the house, she had took a Zoloft she kept hidden just in case of emergencies. She couldn't think of a better moment to utilize it.

Soon after Tamia had made her first round of drink orders, Tanya had arrived. As she walked through the dining area, she took an extended look at each and every inch of the restaurant. She was stunned. The place was beautiful. The whole vibe of it was something new to the area. They approved, so far. She hugged Tamia's neck as she joined her in the booth. Engaging in small talk as they await Salina's arrival, Tamia inquired whether Tanya had heard from Nicholas lately. Surprisingly she had. She shared blushing, that he had actually planned to fly her back to visit him or that he'd come to see her just in case she couldn't get off work. Tanya was glowing, you could tell she really liked this guy. She thought that after her drink encounter with him in Miami that he would want nothing else to do with her. She was happy to learn that it was the complete opposite. Shortly following the arrival of Tanya's drinks and appetizer, Salina had finally waltzed on in. "What's up bitches?" she asked loud and obnoxiously as everyone in the restaurant observed.

"See this is why we can never take you nowhere," Tanya suggested putting her head down embarrassed. "Ouuu, this place is nice," Salina says as she ignores Tanya's comments and looks around the restaurant. "Yes, it's very nice. And also, very quiet," Tamia insinuates. Tanya laughs. Salina joins the ladies sitting on the same side as Tanya facing Tamia. "Where the drinks at?" Salina asks as if expecting they would have ordered for her also before she arrived. Tanya and Tamia both looked at one another in unison and cracked a small grin at the irony. More often than not, they both would go through these phases where they questioned why they were even still friends with Salina. Nothing about Salina complimented the ladies anymore, they honestly just felt like she balanced them all out. They were inseparable during their school days and never had a huge falling out so they managed to remain friends. But at that moment, they were highly annoyed with her presence alone. The waitress returned back to the table to take the rest of their orders. As soon as she walked away, Salina figured it would be best if she did the honors of breaking the ice at the table that evening. Wasting undeniably no time, Salina lead with the hard questions. "Soooo Tamia, what's up with this video going around. Please tell me it's not true?" Tamia looked at her confused. Tanya looked at them both even more confused as if she had been left out of the loop.

"What are you talking about?" "Now you know exactly what I'm talking about." Salina digs her hand into her purse to pull her phone out as if to show Tamia exactly what she was talking about. "This video of you confronting of Shannon and Jarvis." Salina had no filter. Tanya looked at Tamia shocked as if awaiting an explanation.

"The nerve of you bitch asking me about something you claim you heard in a video." Tamia flipped. Her voice quickly changed from melancholy to stern and immense anger. "Damn, bitch. I just asked you a question." The thing is,

Salina honestly didn't think anything of what she asked Tamia nor how she asked it. That was just how she was. Blunt, outspoken, and inconsiderate. She didn't consider the fact that Tamia was married and she was pretty much accusing her of having an affair. She didn't consider the fact that Tamia was a mother and had to maintain a positive representation for her daughter. Neither did she consider the fact that Tamia was her friend and deserved even the slightest of respect and for her to at least approach her in a more discreet and less distasteful manner. Sadly, Salina didn't care. She just wanted to know what she wanted to know.

Between eating an appetizer and a full course meal, the two still managed to continue their argument back and forth until things started to get out of hand. Tanya had to intervene and check Salina about her approach. Of course, Salina did not want to hear it. "Of course, you're defending your leader." Without taking a minute to think before she spoke, she hadn't expected what would follow. Tanya was finished ridiculing herself for the sake of class and self-respect, she slapped Salina right in her face. Salina grabbed her face quickly in shock, she immediately started to have flashbacks. Ever since Salina was in the altercation with the guy from Cheesecake Factory, she had not been the same. She had become more tolerable to people putting her hands on her but also timid. Although not as hard as the guy, Salina was still taken aback by the mere comparability of the two instances. Without hesitation, Salina removed herself from the table and left. Tamia looked at Tanya in amazement. She was happy Tanya had finally stood up for herself, but, she was in as much shock as Salina by the slap on the face. There was a short pause before Tanya looked at Tamia and said, "What? She deserved it." The two shared a laugh. "You slapped the hell out of her girl," Tamia said laughing still surprised. "I'm surprised she didn't hit your ass back." Salina was one never one to walk away from a battle. The mere fact that she held on to her face as soon as Tanya slapped her and didn't instantly hit her back was quite shocking. Salina was one to respond first then apologize later.

"Girl, *and it felt good*," Tanya whispered as if sharing a secret. Tanya had so much bottled up rage in her between the multiple altercations between her and Salina and the non-stop adversity with her ex-husband Rodney. Not to mention the children drove her crazy. She felt a speck of relief.

As the waiter approached the table to collect their plates, Tamia quickly grabbed the menu that she requested to leave on the table earlier. Looking over it briefly, she made another order. Tanya looked at her inquisitively. Tamia had already devoured all 2 plates. Tanya hadn't recalled Tamia eating so much whenever they went out.

"Dang girl, you must be hungry?" Tanya asked rhetorically. "I am; I feel like I'm starving." Tamia said as she shoved her throat with the last of the bread rolls left on the table. Tanya just watched her, thinking what she hadn't yet built up the courage to ask. Pregnancy was a sensitive topic for Tamia. Her and Darnell had been trying to have a baby for the last few years. Apparently, there wasn't a specific reason as to why she hadn't gotten pregnant yet, she just hadn't. Tamia was convinced she couldn't have any more children although she terribly wanted a little boy. On the other hand, Tanya was a nurse and she had plenty of children herself to know the early signs of pregnancy. *'She does seem to have mood swings; she never snaps on Salina like that. Now it seems she's overeating. Then she said she threw up yesterday. If you ask me the girl pregnant,'* Tanya had come to a conclusion.

"You okay?" Tanya asked casually. "If I didn't know any better I'd think you were pregnant." She said with a small chuckle at the end as if she was joking. Tamia looked up at her, barely moving any part of her body besides her eyes. She knew Tanya was aware she loathed the topic of pregnancy unless she was sure she was pregnant. And in this case, Tamia was pretty much sure that was not the case.

"So, because I'm hungry you just automatically assume, I'm pregnant? Girl please." "No, actually because you're craving and eating more than what you usually eat. And because you snapped on Salina. Which you don't usually you do. You usually just be the bigger person and let her have it. You also just said you had thrown up the other day." Tamia forgot she had told them she may not be able to come to dinner that day because she wasn't feeling well. She quickly denied any accusations of pregnant and justified every finding that Tanya had established. The ladies finished up their conversation, shared a hug and left the restaurant after going back and forth between who would pay for Salina's food. She stormed out so quick she hadn't even paid for her food. Tamia convinced Tanya to pay for it as a kind gesture to indicate an apology for slapping her. As friends, no matter how much they wanted to fight one another on several different occasions especially Salina, they had always said they'd never resort to actually putting their hands on each other unless it called for it and they were no longer friends. Tanya and Salina always fought, and always ended up right back friends. Though there was a lot of push back from Tanya, she agreed, paid for the meal, took a picture of her receipt and sent it to Salina.

Tamia daydreamed about the idea of being pregnant all the way home. She had created this whole imaginary life with two children, Darnell and their new beautiful home with a picket fence. She arrived home, immediately started prepping steak, macaroni and cheese, broccoli and Cajun rice. Darnell hadn't gotten home yet after his dinner meeting with colleagues and Talyn was away for the weekend. Her and Darnell were still on bad terms, but she knew cooking up his favorite meal would do just the job to make him forget. She placed everything on then went to take a quick shower. The sound of the door opening and closing had caught her attention- she hadn't expected for Darnell to be home so soon.

"Darnell," Tamia yelled over the sound of the shower to get his attention. No one responded. She yelled his name a second time and the bathroom door opened right away frightening her. He pulled the shower curtain over slightly from the back to get a look at her. "Don't do that. You scared me," she said as she hit him on the shoulder. "My bad baby. It smells good in here." He moved his head closer gesturing for a kiss. She laid a wet one right on him as she licked her lips with saliva. Darnell hated when she did that right before they would kiss, but that time he just let her have it. He smacked her on the but then walked back to the kitchen leaving the bathroom door open.

Tamia stepped out of the shower, with her hair damp just like Darnell preferred, placed her robe on and joined him in the living room. Sitting on his lap, she placed her legs over his rotating to sit on him sideways in the cradle position. Darnell grinned exposing the small dimple in his left cheek.

"What?" Tamia asked blushing.

"Nothing, I can't just stare at my beautiful wife."
"Of course, you can," Tamia started kissing on Darnell's neck. He pulled back her silk robe and returned the gesture. Trying not to release subtle hint of his lips against her neck, she pivoted to wrap her legs around him. The sound of the stove alarm disturbed the two, Tamia had almost forgotten she was cooking.

Darnell followed her to the kitchen and stood over her, rubbing her but as she checked on the food. Tamia could barely keep her composure as she was attempting to take the food out the oven. She gestured with her but, for him to back up. He didn't move a bit; he only took that as a sign of her requesting for me. Tamia preferred that Darnell not stand over her while she was in the kitchen cooking. For some reason she got nervous and felt she couldn't concentrate while anyone was in the kitchen just there, not contributing to the meal being made but just there, like Darnell loved to do. He got the hint and made his way back to the leaving room to put the game on. The food was pretty much done. Tamia made the table and prepared their plates. "C'mon in here and eat babe." She called back over to Darnell inviting him into the dining room to join her for dinner.

"Let's eat in here." Darnell waved her over to join him in the living room. Tamia grabbed the plates and joined him on the couch. Darnell quickly devoured his food as if he hadn't just gotten home from a dinner. He mentioned that he had been finished eating early during the meeting and their dinner consisted more of drinking wine than anything else. Tamia had barely touched her food. She had become so engulfed with just being in the moment that she had forgotten about all that had taken place. In a trance, she stared into space considering whether to tell Darnell or not.

"Babe you okay?" He nudged her, waking her out of her daze. "Yeah, I'm good just not that hungry, I ate not too long ago. Went out to eat with the girls." "Oh, okay." He said.

She went to the kitchen, wrapped her food up and placed it in the refrigerator. She figured she'd be hungry again before the day was over. Darnell watched her walk back towards him. Tamia started to feel shy like a young girl as she noticed the way her husband was watching her. Suddenly she got the sudden urge to puke so she hurriedly took off to the bathroom. Before she had even had the chance to meet the toilet with her face, the puke got a head start and made its way all over the bathroom floor. Darnell was shocked at what he saw as he found her in the bathroom floor on all floors looking back at him as if she was sitting over a dead body.

"Baby, are you okay? What's going on, you sick?" He kneels down to console her. Sweeping her hair behind her ear, he begins to massage her back. Tamia wasn't sure what was going on. She didn't really feel sick, but she also didn't feel well. The thought she may be pregnant never once crossed her mind as a strong possibility but the signs were looking all too familiar for her. It had been almost 8 years since Tamia knew what it was like to be pregnant. Even though she wanted more children, she was daunted by the thought of being pregnant. Not for any specific reason, she just felt that the timing would be all wrong. She sat on the floor in the middle of all of her puke, silent. Darnell felt helpless. He didn't know what was going on with his wife and it seemed she was totally out of it. He picked her up from the floor and carried her over to the bathtub as he ran water for her to get in. "C'mon baby, take your clothes off."

Darnell assisted Tamia in removing her robe and getting into the bathtub. He walked over to the bathroom closet to get a towel. He started cleaning up the floor as Tamia sat in the tub helpless, hopeless. She slowly washed her body with her bath sponge. Once Darnell finished cleaning up the bathroom floor, he proceeded to helping her clean up. He took care of her. Dried her off, wrapped her hair, and placed her in the bed. Though Tamia wasn't feeling well, she was totally capable of taking care of herself. But she was soaking it all in. Darnell came back to bed, lied next to her in the fetal position as he wrapped his arms around her holding her tightly. Tamia snuggled closer to him as Darnell kissed her on the cheek. Their romantic evening alone didn't go as they had planned. He wanted to have sex with her, especially after their last encounter but for some reason he felt uneasy about initiating sex with Tamia seeing as how she might be sick. She stared off into space not even remotely falling to sleep. There was too much weighing on her mind. Everything had literally come down on her all at once and she had a first-class seat to her demise. She just wanted a few more hours if possible, or days without conflict between her and Darnell so she decided against saying anything to him.

Darnell had been wrecking his brain with the thought that something else might be wrong with Tamia. The idea that she may not be sick at all. That there may be absolutely nothing wrong with her and the answer to it all was actually quite obvious. In disbelief, he couldn't get the thought out of his mind that Tamia might actually be pregnant. He recalled when she was pregnant with Talyn and all he could see was her non-stop throwing up which led them to learn that she was pregnant. So, this made perfect since to him-random regurgitation meant pregnancy. He moved his arms from around her, sat up and tapped Tamia on the shoulder gesturing for her to turn around and face him. Though Tamia wasn't sleep it hadn't quite registered yet that she was being tapped. You could hear him exhale deeply as he gathered the words together to ask Tamia what he had been dying to ask her since the moment he saw her lying on the floor in puke appearing perplexed.

"Are you pregnant?"

To Be Continued....

CPSIA information can be obtained
at www.ICGtesting.com
Printed in the USA
LVHW081709120419
613992LV00015B/211/P